WISH YOU WERE HERE

A Novel

Jodi Picoult

BALLANTINE BOOKS

NEW YORK

2022 Ballantine Books Trade Paperback Edition

Published in the United States by Ballantine, an imprint of Random House, a division of Penguin Random House LLC, New York.

BALLANTINE is a registered trademark and the colophon is a trademark of Penguin Random House LLC.
RANDOM HOUSE BOOK CLUB and colophon are trademarks of Penguin Random House LLC.

Originally published in hardcover in the United States by Ballantine, an imprint of Random House, a division of Penguin Random House LLC, in 2021.

This book contains an excerpt from the forthcoming book *Mad Honey* by Jodi Picoult and Jennifer Finney Boylan. This excerpt has been set for this edition only and may not reflect the final content of the forthcoming edition.

Title page and part opener ornament: iStock/mysondanube

LIBRARY OF CONGRESS CATALOGING-IN-PUBLICATION DATA
Names: Picoult, Jodi, author.
Title: Wish you were here: a novel / Jodi Picoult.
Description: First Edition. | New York: Ballantine Books, [2021]
Identifiers: LCCN 2021027370 (print) | LCCN 2021027371 (ebook) |
ISBN 9781984818430 (trade paperback) | ISBN 9780593497203 (international edition) |
9781984818423 (ebook)
Classification: LCC PS3566.I372 W57 2021 (print) | LCC PS3566.I372 (ebook) |
DDC 813/.54—dc23
LC record available at https://lccn.loc.gov/2021027370
LC ebook record available at https://lccn.loc.gov/2021027371

Printed in the United States of America on acid-free paper

randomhousebooks.com
randomhousebookclub.com

2 4 6 8 9 7 5 3 1

Book design by Caroline Cunningham

WISH

YOU

WERE

HERE

"There are some writers who just have a knack for writing about resilience and the human spirit—especially in moments of crises. Jodi Picoult is one of those writers. Her research is meticulous. . . . A deeply moving novel about plowing through darkness to find the light—in a pandemic."

—*She Reads*

"An emotional and heart-wrenching read with a twist or two that will keep readers riveted to the page."

—*BookBub*

"Gather around and prepare to once again be reduced to a sobbing mess by the bestselling author."

—*E! Online*

"An early and triumphant addition to books trying to make sense of life in 2020, and beyond."

—*Business Insider*

"Crafting a pandemic novel is a huge undertaking, given what we've all experienced in the last two years, but there is no novelist I trust more."

—*Off the Shelf*

"A beautifully written novel."

—Lisa Scottoline

"Jodi Picoult once again proves she is the master of wading through the darkness to find the light. *Wish You Were Here* is a powerfully evocative story of resilience and the triumph of the human spirit."

—Taylor Jenkins Reid, *New York Times* bestselling author of *Malibu Rising*

"*Wish You Were Here* is a transporting and transcendent novel about seeking out glimmers of light in the darkness, and following them wherever they lead. Jodi Picoult is that rare, one-in-a-million writer whose books both squeeze your heart and expand your mind. Her latest is wise, surprising, and utterly extraordinary."

—EMILY HENRY, #1 *New York Times* bestselling author of
People We Meet on Vacation and *Beach Read*

"In *Wish You Were Here*, Jodi Picoult does something brilliant, cracking open something extraordinary. I am just overwhelmed by this book. I actually finished it at three in the morning and started reading it again."

—CAROLINE LEAVITT, *New York Times* bestselling
author of *With or Without You*

For Melanie Borinstein, soon to be the newest member of our family.

There's no one else I'd rather run a quarantine salon with.

According to Darwin's *Origin of Species,* it is not the most intellectual of the species that survives; it is not the strongest that survives; but the species that survives is the one that is able best to adapt and adjust to the changing environment in which it finds itself.

—LEON C. MEGGINSON

ONE

ONE

March 13, 2020

When I was six years old, I painted a corner of the sky. My father was working as a conservator, one of a handful restoring the zodiac ceiling on the main hall of Grand Central Terminal—an aqua sky strung with shimmering constellations. It was late, way past my bedtime, but my father took me to work because my mother—as usual—was not home.

He helped me carefully climb the scaffolding, where I watched him working on a cleaned patch of the turquoise paint. I looked at the stars representing the smear of the Milky Way, the golden wings of Pegasus, Orion's raised club, the twisted fish of Pisces. The original mural had been painted in 1913, my father told me. Roof leaks damaged the plaster, and in 1944, it had been replicated on panels that were attached to the arched ceiling. The original plan had been to remove the boards for restoration, but they contained asbestos, and so the conservators left them in place, and went to work with cotton swabs and cleaning solution, erasing decades of pollutants.

They uncovered history. Signatures and inside jokes and notes left behind by the original artists were revealed, tucked in among the constellations. There were dates commemorating weddings, and the end of World War II. There were names of soldiers. The birth of twins was recorded near Gemini.

An error had been made by the original artists, so that the painted zodiac was reversed from the way it would appear in the night sky. Instead of correcting it, though, my father was diligently reinforcing the error. That night, he was working on a small square of space, gilding stars. He had already painted over the tiny yellow dots with adhesive. He covered these with a piece of gold leaf, light as breath. Then he turned to me. "Diana," he said, holding out his hand, and I climbed up in front of him, caged by the safety of his body. He handed me a brush to sweep over the foil, fixing it in place. He showed me how to gently rub at it with my thumb, so that the galaxy he'd created was all that remained.

When all the work was finished, the conservators kept a small dark spot in the northwest corner of Grand Central Terminal, where the pale blue ceiling meets the marble wall. This nine-by-five-inch section was left that way intentionally. My father told me that conservators do that, in case historians need to study the original composition. The only way you can tell how far you've come is to know where you started.

Every time I'm in Grand Central Terminal, I think about my father. Of how we left that night, hand in hand, our palms glittering like we had stolen the stars.

It is Friday the thirteenth, so I should know better. Getting from Sotheby's, on the Upper East Side, to the Ansonia, on the Upper West Side, means taking the Q train to Times Square and then the 1 uptown, so I have to travel in the wrong direction before I start going in the right one.

I *hate* going backward.

Normally I would walk across Central Park, but I am wearing a new pair of shoes that are rubbing a blister on my heel, shoes I never would have worn if I'd known that I was going to be summoned by Kitomi Ito. So instead, I find myself on public transit. But something's off, and it takes me a moment to figure out what.

It's quiet. Usually, I have to fight my way through tourists who are listening to someone singing for coins, or a violin quartet. Today, though, the platform is empty.

Last night Broadway theaters had shut down performances for a month, after an usher tested positive for Covid, out of an abundance of caution. That's what Finn said, anyway—New York–Presbyterian, where he is a resident, has not seen the influx of coronavirus cases that are appearing in Washington State and Italy and France. There were only nineteen cases in the city, Finn told me last night as we watched the news, when I wondered out loud if we should start panicking yet. "Wash your hands and don't touch your face," he told me. "It's going to be fine."

The uptown subway is nearly empty, too. I get off at Seventy-second and emerge aboveground, blinking like a mole, walking at a brisk New Yorker clip. The Ansonia, in all its glory, rises up like an angry djinn, defiantly jutting its Beaux Arts chin at the sky. For a moment, I just stand on the sidewalk, looking up at its mansard roof and its lazy sprawl from Seventy-third to Seventy-fourth Street. There's a North Face and an American Apparel at ground level, but it wasn't always this bougie. Kitomi told me that when she and Sam Pride moved in in the seventies, the building was overrun with psychics and mediums, and housed a swingers' club with an orgy room and an open bar and buffet. *Sam and I,* she said, *would stop in at least once a week.*

I was not alive when Sam's band, the Nightjars, was formed by Sam and his co-songwriter, William Punt, with two school chums from Slough, England. Nor was I when their first album spent thirty weeks on the *Billboard* charts, or when their little British quartet went on *The Ed Sullivan Show* and ignited a stampede of screaming American girls. Not when Sam married Kitomi Ito ten years later or when the band broke up, months after their final album was released featuring cover art of Kitomi and Sam naked, mirroring the figures in a painting that hung behind their bed. And I wasn't alive when Sam was murdered three years later, on the steps of this very building, stabbed in the throat by a mentally ill man who recognized him from that iconic album cover.

But like everyone else on the planet, I know the whole story.

The doorman at the Ansonia smiles politely at me; the concierge looks up as I approach. "I'm here to see Kitomi Ito," I say coolly, pushing my license across the desk to her.

"She's expecting you," the concierge answers. "Floor—"

"Eighteen. I know."

Lots of celebrities have lived at the Ansonia—from Babe Ruth to Theodore Dreiser to Toscanini to Natalie Portman—but arguably, Kitomi and Sam Pride are the most famous. If my husband had been murdered on the front steps of my apartment building, I might not have stayed for another thirty years, but that's just me. And anyway, Kitomi is finally moving now, which is why the world's most infamous rock widow has my number in her cellphone.

What is my life, I think, as I lean against the back wall of the elevator.

When I was young, and people asked what I wanted to do when I grew up, I had a whole plan. I wanted to be securely on a path to my career, to get married by thirty, to finish having kids by thirty-five. I wanted to speak fluent French and have traveled cross-country on Route 66. My father had laughed at my checklist. *You,* he told me, *are definitely your mother's daughter.*

I did not take that as a compliment.

Also, for the record, I'm perfectly on track. I am an associate specialist at Sotheby's—*Sotheby's!*—and Eva, my boss, has hinted in all ways possible that after the auction of Kitomi's painting I will likely be promoted. I am not engaged, but when I ran out of clean socks last weekend and went to scrounge for a pair of Finn's, I found a ring hidden in the back of his underwear drawer. We leave tomorrow on vacation and Finn's going to pop the question there. I'm so sure of it that I got a manicure today instead of eating lunch.

And I'm twenty-nine.

The door to the elevator opens directly into Kitomi's foyer, all black and white marble squares like a giant chessboard. She comes into the entryway, dressed in jeans and combat boots and a pink silk bathrobe, with a thatch of white hair and the purple heart-shaped spectacles for which she is known. She has always reminded me of a wren, light and hollow-boned. I think of how Kitomi's black hair went white overnight with grief after Sam was murdered. I think of the photographs of her on the sidewalk, gasping for air.

"Diana!" she says, as if we are old friends.

There is a brief awkwardness as I instinctively put my hand out to take hers and then remember that is not a thing we are doing anymore and instead just give a weird little wave. "Hi, Kitomi," I say.

"I'm so glad you could come today."

"It's not a problem. There are a lot of sellers who want to make sure the paperwork is handed over personally."

Over her shoulder, at the end of a long hallway, I can see it—the Toulouse-Lautrec painting that is the entire reason I know Kitomi Ito. She sees my eyes dart toward it and her mouth tugs into a smile.

"I can't help it," I say. "I never get tired of seeing it."

A strange flicker crosses Kitomi's face. "Then let's get you a better view," she replies, and she leads me deeper into her home.

From 1892 to 1895, Henri de Toulouse-Lautrec scandalized the impressionist art world by moving into a brothel and painting prostitutes together in bed. *Le Lit*, one of the most famous in that series, is at the Musée d'Orsay. Others have been sold to private collections for ten million and twelve million dollars. The painting in Kitomi's house is clearly part of the series and yet patently set apart from the others.

There are not two women in this one, but a woman and a man. The woman sits propped up naked against the headboard, the sheet fallen to her waist. Behind the headboard is a mirror, and in it you can see the reflection of the second figure in the painting—Toulouse-Lautrec himself, seated naked at the foot of the bed with sheets pooled in his lap, his back to the viewer as he stares as intently at the woman as she is staring at him. It's intimate and voyeuristic, simultaneously private and public.

When the Nightjars released their final album, *Twelfth of Never*, the cover art had Kitomi bare-breasted against their headboard, gazing at Sam, whose broad back forms the lower third of the visual field. Behind their bed hangs the painting they're emulating, in the position the mirror holds in the actual art.

Everyone knows that album cover. Everyone knows that Sam bought this painting for Kitomi from a private collection, as a wedding gift.

But only a handful of people know that she is now selling it, at a unique Sotheby's auction, and that I'm the one who closed that deal.

"Are you still going on vacation?" Kitomi asks, disrupting my reverie.

Did I tell her about our trip? Maybe. But I cannot think of any logical reason she would care.

Clearing my throat (I don't get paid to moon over art, I get paid to transact it), I paste a smile on my face. "Only for two weeks, and then the minute I get back, it's full steam ahead for your auction." My job is a strange one—I have to convince clients to give their beloved art up for adoption, which is a careful dance between rhapsodizing over the piece and encouraging them that they are doing the right thing by selling it. "If you're having any anxiety about the transfer of the painting to our offices, don't," I tell her. "I promise that I will personally be here overseeing the crating, and I'll be there on the other end, too." I glance back at the canvas. "We're going to find this the perfect home," I vow. "So. The paperwork?"

Kitomi glances out the window before turning back to me. "About that," she says.

"What do you mean, she doesn't want to sell?" Eva says, looking at me over the rims of her famous horn-rimmed glasses. Eva St. Clerck is my boss, my mentor, and a legend. As the head of sale for the Imp Mod auction—the giant sale of impressionist and modern art—she is who I'd like to be by the time I'm forty, and until this moment, I had firmly enjoyed being teacher's pet, tucked under the wing of her expertise.

Eva narrows her eyes. "I knew it. Someone from Christie's got to her."

In the past, Kitomi has sold other pieces of art with Christie's, the main competitor of Sotheby's. To be fair, everyone assumed that was how she'd sell the Toulouse-Lautrec, too . . . until I did something I never should have done as an associate specialist, and convinced her otherwise.

"It's not Christie's—"

"Phillips?" Eva asks, her eyebrows arching.

"No. None of them. She just wants to take a pause," I clarify. "She's concerned about the virus."

"Why?" Eva asks, dumbfounded. "It's not like a painting can catch it."

"No, but buyers can at an auction."

"Well, I can talk her down from that ledge," Eva says. "We've got firm interest from the Clooneys and Beyoncé and Jay-Z, for God's sake."

"Kitomi's also nervous because the stock market's tanking. She thinks things are going to get worse, fast. And she wants to wait it out a bit . . . be safe not sorry."

Eva rubs her temples. "You do realize we've already leaked this sale," she says. "*The New Yorker* literally did a feature on it."

"She just needs a little more time," I say.

Eva glances away, already dismissing me in her mind. "You can go," she orders.

I step out of her office and into the maze of hallways, lined with the books that I've used to research art. I've been at Sotheby's for six and a half years—seven if you count the internship I did when I was still at Williams College. I went straight from undergrad into their master's program in art business. I started out as a graduate trainee, then became a junior cataloger in the Impressionist Department, doing initial research for incoming paintings. I would study what else the artist was working on around the same time and how much similar works sold for, sometimes writing up the first draft of the catalog blurb. Though the rest of the world is digital these days, the art world still produces physical catalogs that are beautiful and glossy and nuanced and very, very important. Now, as an associate specialist,

I perform other tasks for Eva: visiting the artwork in situ and noting any imperfections, the same way you look over a rental car for dings before you sign the contract; physically accompanying the painting as it is packed up and moved from a home to our office; and occasionally joining my boss for meetings with potential clients.

A hand snakes out of a doorway I am passing and grabs my shoulder, pulling me into a little side room. "Jesus," I say, nearly falling into Rodney—my best friend here at Sotheby's. Like me, he started as a college intern. Unlike me, he did not wind up going into the business side of the auction house. Instead, he designs and helps create the spaces where the art is showcased for auction.

"Is it true?" Rodney asks. "Did you lose the Nightjars' painting?"

"First, it's not the Nightjars' painting. It's Kitomi Ito's. Second, how the *hell* did you find out so fast?"

"Honey, rumor is the lifeblood of this entire industry," Rodney says. "And it spreads through these halls faster than the flu." He hesitates. "Or coronavirus, as it may be."

"Well, I didn't *lose* the Toulouse-Lautrec. Kitomi just wants things to settle down first."

Rodney folds his arms. "You think that's happening anytime soon? The mayor declared a state of emergency yesterday."

"Finn said there are only nineteen cases in the city," I tell him.

Rodney looks at me like I've just said I still believe in Santa, with a mixture of disbelief and pity. "You can have one of my rolls of toilet paper," he says.

For the first time, I look behind him. There are six different shades of gold paint rolled onto the walls. "Which do you like?" he asks.

I point to one stripe in the middle. "Really?" he says, squinting. "What's it for?"

"A display of medieval manuscripts. Private sale."

"Then that one," I say, nodding at the stripe beside it. Which looks exactly the same. "Come up to Sant Ambroeus with me," I beg. It's the café at the top of Sotheby's, and there is a prosciutto and mozzarella sandwich there that might erase the look on Eva's face from my mind.

"Can't. It's popcorn for me today."

The break room has free microwave popcorn, and on busy days, that's lunch. "Rodney," I hear myself say, "I'm screwed."

He settles his hands on my shoulders, spinning me and walking me toward the opposite wall, where a mirrored panel is left over from the previous installation. "What do you see?"

I look at my hair, which has always been too red for my taste, and my eyes, steel blue. My lipstick has worn off. My skin is a ghostly winter white. And there's a weird stain on the collar of my blouse. "I see someone who can kiss her promotion goodbye."

"Funny," Rodney says, "because I see someone who is going on vacation tomorrow and who should have zero fucks left to give about Kitomi Ito or Eva St. Clerck or Sotheby's. Think about tropical drinks and paradise and playing doctor with your boyfriend—"

"Real doctors don't do that—"

"—and snorkeling with Gila monsters—"

"Marine iguanas."

"Whatever." Rodney squeezes me from behind, meeting my gaze in the mirror. "Diana, by the time you get back here in two weeks, everyone will have moved on to another scandal." He smirks at me. "Now go buy some SPF 50 and get out of here."

I laugh as Rodney picks up a paint roller and smoothly covers all the gold stripes with the one I picked. Once, he told me that an auction house wall can have a foot of paint on it, because they are repainted constantly.

As I close the door behind me, I wonder what color this room first was, and if anyone here even remembers.

To get to Hastings-on-Hudson, a commuter town north of the city, you can take Metro-North from Grand Central. So for the second time today, I head to Midtown.

This time, though, I visit the main concourse of the building and position myself directly underneath the piece of sky I painted with my father, letting my gaze run over the backward zodiac and the freckles of stars that blush across the arch of the ceiling. Craning my neck back, I stare until I'm dizzy, until I can almost hear my father's voice again.

It's been four years since he died, and the only way I can garner the courage to visit my mother is to come here first, as if his memory gives me protective immunity.

I am not entirely sure why I'm going to see her. It's not like she asked for me. And it's not like this is part of any routine. I haven't been to visit in three months, actually.

Maybe *that's* why I'm going.

The Greens is an assisted living facility walkable from the train station in Hastings-on-Hudson—which is one of the reasons I picked it, when my mother reappeared out of the blue after years of radio silence. And, naturally, she didn't show up oozing maternal warmth. She was a problem that needed to be solved.

The building is made out of brick and fits into a community that looks like it was cut and pasted from New England. Trees line the street, and there's a library next door. Cobblestones arch in a widening circle from the front door. It isn't until you are buzzed in through the locked door and see the color-coded hallways and the photographs on the residents' apartment doors that you realize it's a memory care facility.

I sign in and walk past a woman shuffling into the bright art room, filled with all sorts of paints and clay and crafts. As far as I know, my mother has never participated.

They do all kinds of things here to make it easier for the occupants. Doorways meant to be entered by the residents have bright yellow frames they cannot miss; rooms for staff or storage blend into the walls, painted over with murals of bookshelves or greenery. Since all the apartment doors look similar, there's a large photo on each one that has meaning to the person who lives there: a family member, a special location, a beloved pet. In my mother's case, it's one of her own most famous photographs—a refugee who's come by raft from Cuba, carrying the limp body of his dehydrated son in his arms. It's grotesque and grim and the pain radiates from the image. In other words, exactly the kind of photo for which Hannah O'Toole was known.

There is a punch code that opens the secure unit on both sides of the door. (The keypad on the inside is always surrounded by a small zombie clot of residents trying to peer over your shoulder to see the numbers and presumably the path to freedom.) The individual rooms aren't locked. When I let myself into my mother's room, the space is neat and uncluttered. The television is on—the television is *always* on—tuned to a game show. My mother sits on the couch with her hands in her lap, like she's at a cotillion waiting to be asked to dance.

She is younger than most of the residents here. There's one skunk streak of white in her black hair, but it's been there since I was little. She doesn't really look much different from the way she did when I was a girl, except for her stillness. My mother was always in motion—talking animatedly with her hands, turning at the next question, adjusting the lens of a camera, hieing away from us to some corner of the globe to capture a revolution or a natural disaster.

Beyond her is the screened porch, the reason that I picked The Greens. I thought that someone who'd spent so much of her life outdoors would hate the confinement of a memory care facility. The screened porch was safe, because there was no egress from it, but it allowed a view. Granted, it was only a strip of lawn and beyond that a parking lot, but it was something.

It costs a shitload of money to keep my mother here. When she showed up on my doorstep, in the company of two police officers who found her wandering around Central Park in a bathrobe, I hadn't even known she was back in the city. They found my address in her wallet, torn from the corner of an old Christmas card envelope. *Ma'am,* one of the officers had asked me, *do you know this woman?*

I recognized her, of course. But I didn't *know* her at all.

When it became clear that my mother had dementia, Finn asked me what I was going to do. *Nothing,* I told him. She had barely been involved in taking care of me when I was young; why was I obligated to take care of her now? I remember seeing the look on his face when he realized that for me, maybe, love was a quid pro quo. I didn't want to ever see that expression again on Finn, but I also knew my limitations, and I didn't have the resources to become the caretaker for someone with early-onset Alzheimer's. So I did my due diligence, talking to her neurologist and getting pamphlets from different facilities. The Greens was the best of the lot, but it was expensive. In the end, I packed up my mother's apartment, Sotheby's auctioned off the photographs from her walls, and the result was an annuity that could pay for her new residence.

I did not miss the irony of the fact that the parent I missed desperately was the one who was no longer in the world, while the parent I could take or leave was inextricably tied to me for the long haul.

Now, I paste a smile on my face and sit down next to my mother on the couch. I can count on two hands the number of times I've come to visit since installing her here, but I very clearly remember the directions of the staff: act like she knows you, and even if she doesn't remember, she will likely follow the social cues and treat you like a friend. The first time I'd come, when she asked who I was and I said *Your daughter,* she had become so agitated that she'd bolted away, fallen over a chair, and cut her forehead.

"Who's winning *Wheel of Fortune*?" I ask, settling in as if I'm a regular visitor.

Her eyes dart toward me. There's a flicker of confusion, like a sputtering pilot light, before she smooths it away. "The lady in the pink shirt," my mother says. Her brows draw together, as she tries to place me. "Are you—"

"The last time I was here, it was warm outside," I interrupt, offering the clue that this isn't the first time I've visited. "It's pretty warm out today. Should we open the slider?"

She nods, and I walk toward the entrance to the screened porch. The latch that locks it from the inside is open. "You're supposed to keep this fastened," I remind her. I don't have to worry about her wandering off—but it still makes me nervous to have the sliding door unlocked.

"Are we going somewhere?" she asks, when a gust of fresh air blows into the living room.

"Not today," I tell her. "But I'm taking a trip tomorrow. To the Galápagos."

"I've been there," my mother says, lighting up as a thread of memory catches. "There's a tortoise. Lonesome George. He's the last of his whole species. Imagine being the last of anything in the whole world."

For some reason, my throat thickens with tears. "He died," I say.

My mother tilts her head. "Who?"

"Lonesome George."

"Who's George?" she asks, and she narrows her eyes. "Who are *you*?"

That sentence, it wounds me.

I don't know why it hurts so much when my mother forgets me these days, though, when she never actually knew me at all.

When Finn comes home from the hospital, I am in bed under the covers wearing my favorite flannel shirt and sweatpants, with my laptop balanced on my legs. Today has just *flattened* me. Finn sits down beside me, leaning against the headboard. His golden hair is wet, which means he's showered before coming home from New York–Presbyterian, where he is a resident in the surgery department, but he's wearing scrubs that show off the curves of his biceps and the constellation of freckles on his arms. He glances at the screen, and then at the empty pint of ice cream nestled beside me. "Wow," he says. "*Out of Africa . . . and* butter pecan? That's, like, the big guns."

I lean my head on his shoulder. "I had the shittiest day."

"No, I did," Finn replies.

"I lost a painting," I tell him.

"I lost a patient."

I groan. "You win. You always win. No one ever dies of an art emergency."

Her wide black eyes blink. "My brother?" she says, and then she huffs a sharp laugh. "He is *not* my brother. And it doesn't really matter if he knows or not. It's an island. How far away could I even get?"

When I was in school and that girl was harming herself, I felt like our paths kept crossing. Probably they had before, too, but I hadn't been aware. One day, as we passed in the hallway, I stopped her. *You shouldn't do it,* I said. *You could really hurt yourself.*

She had laughed at me. *That's the point.*

I watch this girl pick up a few more plastic bottles and jam them into her bag. "You speak English so well."

She glances at me. "I'm aware."

"I didn't mean—" I hesitate, trying to not say something inadvertently offensive. "It's just nice to have someone to talk to." I reach down and grab a bottle, holding it out for her bag. "I'm Diana," I say.

"Beatriz."

Up close, she seems older than I first thought. Maybe fourteen or fifteen, but petite, with sharp features and bottomless eyes. She is still wearing her sweatshirt, arms pulled low beyond her wrists. There is a school crest over her heart. She seems perfectly content to ignore me, and maybe I should respect that. But I am lonely, and just days ago, I watched her self-harming. Maybe I am not the only one who needs someone to talk to.

I also know, based on our previous interactions, that she is more likely to flee than to confide in me. So I choose my words carefully, like holding out a crust of bread to a bird and wondering if it will dart away, or hop one step closer. "Do you always pick up the trash here?" I ask casually.

"Someone has to," she says.

I think about that, about all the visitors, like me, who descend on the Galápagos. Economically, I'm sure it's a boon. But maybe having all the boats and tours suspended for a few weeks isn't a bad thing. Maybe it gives nature a moment to breathe.

"So," I say, making conversation. "Is that your school?" I point to my chest, in the same spot where the logo is on her sweatshirt. "Tomás de Berlanga?"

She nods. "It's on Santa Cruz, but it shut down because of the virus."

"So that's where you live?"

She starts walking; I fall into place beside her. "During the school year I live with a family in Santa Cruz," she says quietly. "*Lived* with."

"But this is where you were born?" I guess.

Beatriz turns to me. "I do not belong here."

Neither do I, I think.

I follow her further down the beach. "So you're on vacation."

She snorts. "Yeah. Like *you're* on vacation."

Her barb hits home; as holidays go, this isn't exactly what I hoped for. "How come you go to school off-island?"

"I've been there since I was nine. It's like a magnet school. My mother enrolled me because it was the best chance of getting me out of Galápagos forever, and because it was the last thing my father wanted."

It makes me think of my own mother and father. Separate circles that didn't even overlap to form a Venn diagram where I could nestle into both their spaces.

"He's your father," I guess. "Gabriel?"

Beatriz looks at me. "Unfortunately."

I try to do the math; he seems so young to be her parent. He can't be much older than I am.

She starts walking away. "Why was he yelling at you?" I ask.

She turns. "Why are you following me?"

"I'm not . . ." Except, I realize, I am. "I'm sorry. I just . . . I haven't had a conversation with anyone in a few days. I don't speak Spanish."

"Americana," she mutters.

"I wasn't planning on coming here alone. My boyfriend had to back out at the last minute."

This, she finds intriguing; I can see it in her eyes. "He had to work," I explain. "He's a doctor."

"Why did you stay, then?" she asks. "When you found out the island was closing?"

Why *did* I? It's been only a few days, but I can barely remember. Because I thought it was the adventurous thing to do?

"If I had anywhere else to go, I would," Beatriz says.

"Why?"

She laughs, but it's bitter. "I hate Isabela. Plus, my father expects me to live in a half-finished shack on our farm."

"He's a *farmer*?" I say, my surprise slipping out.

"He used to be a tour guide, but not anymore."

Likely, I think, *because he was so unpleasant to his clientele.*

"My grandfather owned the business, but when he died, my father closed it down. He used to live in the apartment you're in, but he moved to the highlands, to a place without water or electricity or internet—"

"Internet? There's internet on this island?" I hold up the postcard I am still clutching. "I can't send email, and I haven't been able to call my boyfriend, either . . . so I was writing him. But I can't buy stamps . . . and I don't even know if there's still mail service . . ."

Beatriz holds out her hand. "Give me your phone." I hold it out, and she taps through the settings. "The hotel has Wi-Fi." She nods toward a building in the distance. "I put in their password—but it shits out more often than it works, and if they're closed, they probably turned off the modem. If you still can't connect, you could try getting a SIM card in town."

I take back my phone, and Beatriz reaches for another bottle. A rogue wave soaks her arm, and she pushes her sleeve up before she remembers the red weals left by the razor blade. Immediately, she claps her palm over them, and juts her chin up as if daring me to comment.

"Thank you," I say carefully. "For talking to me."

She shrugs.

"If you wanted to, you know, talk . . . again . . ." My eyes flicker to her arm. "Well, I'm not going anywhere in the near future."

Her face shutters. "I'm good," she says, yanking down the wet fabric. She looks at the postcard, still in my hand. "I could mail it for you."

"Really?"

She shrugs. "We have stamps. I don't know about the post office, but fishermen are allowed off-island to deliver what they catch, so maybe they're taking mail to Santa Cruz."

"That would be . . ." I smile at her. "That would be amazing."

"No big deal. Well. Gotta go check in with the warden."

When I glance up, I realize we have walked all the way to town.

"Your father?" I clarify.

"Tanto monta, monta tanto," she says.

I wonder if the reason Gabriel is keeping such a tight rein on Beatriz is because he knows she's cutting. I wonder if he isn't angry, but desperate.

"Could you stay with your mom instead?" I blurt out.

Beatriz shakes her head. "She's been gone since I was ten."

Heat rushes to my face. "I'm so sorry," I murmur.

She laughs. "She's not dead. She's on a Nat Geo tour ship in Baja, fucking her boyfriend. Good riddance." Without saying another word, Beatriz slings the bag over her shoulder and walks down the middle of the main street, scattering startled iguanas in her wake.

The proprietor of Sonny's Sunnies speaks English and sells more than sunglasses and sarongs. She also sells T-shirts and neon-bright bikinis and SD cards for cameras and, yes, SIM cards for international calling—although there are none in stock at the moment. I can't believe my continued streak of bad luck. She's right there where Beatriz said I'd find her, on the main street of Puerto Villamil, just before noon. The door is wide open and Sonny is sitting behind the cash register, fanning herself with a magazine. She is round everywhere—her face, her arms, her swollen belly—and she peers at me over an embroidered mask. *"Tienes que usar una mascarilla,"* she says, and I just stare at her. The only word I understand in her sentence sounds like eye makeup, and I'm not wearing any.

"I . . . *no habla español,*" I stammer, and her eyes light up.

"Oh," she says, "you're the *turista*." She points to her face. "You need a mask."

I glance around the store. "I need more than that," I tell her, making a small pile on the counter—Galápagos tees, two pairs of shorts, a sweatshirt, a bikini, a face mask made of cloth with little chili peppers printed on it. I add a guidebook with a map of Isabela. When I show her my phone, she shows me a SIM card that will let me make local calls on a local network, which I buy even though I can't imagine who I'll be calling or texting locally. No, she tells me, she doesn't sell stamps.

Finally, I pull out a credit card. "Do you know where there's an ATM on the island?"

"Oh," she says, putting my card in one of those old machines that create a carbon copy of it. "There's no ATM."

"Not even at the bank?"

"No. And you can't use a credit card there to get cash."

I look at the minuscule amount of money I have left, after paying Abuela—thirty-three dollars. Minus ferry fare returning to Santa Cruz . . . as I do the math, my heart starts pounding. What if my cash supply doesn't last me for another week and a half?

My panic attack is interrupted by the jingle of the bell on the door. In walks another woman in a mask, carrying a toddler. He squirms in her arms, calling out to the shop owner until he is set down on the floor and races toward her, clinging to her leg like a mollusk. She swings him onto her hip.

The woman who carried in the little boy unleashes a torrent of words I cannot understand and then she seems to notice me.

She looks familiar, but I can't figure out why until she snaps toward the proprietor, and her long, black braid whips behind her. The woman from my hotel, whose name tag read Elena. Who told me they were closed.

"You are still here?" she says.

"I'm staying with . . . Abuela," I reply. That means *grandmother*, I know. I'm embarrassed to not know her real name.

"*La plena!*" Elena scoffs, throws up her hands, and slams out of the store.

"You're staying in Gabriel Fernandez's old place?" the shop owner asks, and when I nod, she laughs. "Elena's just pissed because *she* wanted to be the one sleeping in his bed."

I feel my cheeks heat. "I'm not . . . I don't . . ." I shake my head. "I have a boyfriend at home."

"Okay," she says, shrugging.

To: DOToole@gmail.com
From: FColson@nyp.org

I keep checking my phone to see if you've texted. I know it isn't your fault, but I wish I knew for sure you are okay. Plus, I need some good news.

This virus is like a storm that just won't ease up. You know on some rational level that it can't stay like this forever. Except, it does. And gets worse.

The easy-to-diagnose Covid patient has fever, chest pain, a cough, a loss of smell and a metallic taste in their mouth, hypoxia, and fear.

The ones that aren't as obvious arrive with abdominal pain and vomiting.

The ones you get Covid from have no symptoms and go to the ER because they cut their hands slicing a bagel.

My attending said we should assume everyone in the hospital has Covid.

He's pretty much right.

But weirdly, the ER isn't very busy. No one's just *walking in* anymore, they're too scared. You never know if the guy with the broken leg sitting next to you in the ER is Covid-positive and asymptomatic. God forbid you cough, even if you have a common cold. You'll be looked at like you're a terrorist.

Since no one wants to risk coming to the hospital, most of the patients arrive by ambulance, coming only when they're unable to breathe.

I've been assigned to one of the Covid ICUs. It's loud AF. There are beeps and alarms that go off any time a vital sign changes. The ventilator makes a noise every time it breathes for a patient. But there are no visitors. It's weird for there to be no crying wives or family members holding a patient's hand.

Oh, and every day, treatment changes. Today we're giving hydroxychloroquine. Tomorrow: whoops, no, we're not. Today we're trying remdesivir, but antibiotics are out. One attending is pushing Lipitor, because it lowers inflammation. Another's trying Lasix, used for heart failure patients, to help remove fluid from around Covid lungs. Some docs think ibuprofen is doing more harm than good, although no one knows why, so they're giving Tylenol for fever instead. Everyone wants to know if convalescent plasma helps, but we don't have enough of it to know.

When I'm not with a patient, I'm reading studies to see what other docs are doing in other places, and what clinical trials are available. It's like we're throwing shit at a wall to see if anything sticks.

Today, I had a patient who was bleeding through her lungs. Normally, we'd give a thousand milligrams of steroids to stop the hemorrhage, but my attending was waffling, because based on previous flu studies, we're worried that steroids might make Covid worse. I kept watching him wrestle with a course of action, and all I could think was: does it matter, if she's dead either way?

But I didn't say anything. I left the room and did my rounds, listening to lungs that couldn't push air and hearts that barely were beating, checking vitals and fluid status, hoping that the patients I was checking on could ride out the virus before we run out of beds. There is a thousand-bed Navy ship being sent to NYC but it won't get here till April; and based on estimates, the hospitals in the city will max out of beds in 45 days.

It's only been a week.

I decided I'm not listening to the news anymore, because I'm basically living it.

God, I wish you were here.

In 2014, one of the plaster rosettes fell from the ceiling of the Rose Main Reading Room of the New York Public Library and shattered on the floor. When the city decided to inspect it, they also inspected the ceiling in the adjacent Blass Catalog Room. The ornate plaster-work of that ceiling was touched up and tested for weight and strength. The 1911 James Wall Finn trompe l'oeil mural of the sky on canvas, however, couldn't be restored because it was too fragile. In-stead, my father spent nearly a year re-creating the image on canvas that would be set in place on the ceiling, and could be easily removed for touch-ups in the future.

When the canvases were being installed in 2016, he was there directing the operation. Because he was a perfectionist, he insisted on climbing up a ladder to illustrate how the edge of the canvas had to align, flush, with the gilded satyrs and cherubs of the carving that framed it.

That same day, I was in East Hampton, at the second home of a woman who was auctioning off a Matisse with Sotheby's. Our pro-tocol required someone from the auction house to be present when a piece was transported, and since I had just been promoted to a junior specialist in Imp Mod, I was given the assignment. It was mindless work. I would take a company car to the site, meet the shipping com-pany there, and before it was packed up I'd use a printed copy of the painting to mark down any scratches or peels or imperfections. I'd oversee the careful packing of the piece, watch it get loaded into a truck, and then I would get back into my company car and return to the office.

The job, however, was not going according to plan. Although our client had said her housekeeper would be expecting us, her husband was also home. He'd had no idea that his wife was selling the Matisse, and he didn't want to. He kept insisting that I show him the contract, and when I did, he told me he was going to call his lawyer, and I suggested he should maybe call his wife instead.

The whole time, my phone was buzzing in my pocket.

When I finally answered, the number was not one I recognized.

Is this Diana O'Toole?

I'm Margaret Wu, I'm a doctor at Mount Sinai . . .

I'm afraid your father's been in an accident.

I walked out of the house in the Hamptons, dazed, completely oblivious to the man still on the phone with his lawyer and the movers awaiting my approval to wrap up the painting. I got into the company car and directed the driver to take me to Mount Sinai. I called Finn, whom I'd been dating for several months, and he said he'd meet me there.

My father had fallen off a ladder and struck his head. He was hemorrhaging in his brain, and had been taken directly into surgery. I wanted to be there holding his hand; I wanted to tell him it was going to be all right. I wanted my face to be the first thing he saw in the recovery room.

The traffic on Long Island was, as usual, a disaster. As I cried in the backseat of the company car, I bargained with a higher power. *I will give You anything,* I swore, *if You get me to the hospital before my father wakes up.*

Finn stood up as soon as I walked through the sliding glass doors, and I *knew.* I could tell from the look on his face and the speed with which he wrapped his arms around me. *There was nothing you could have done,* he whispered.

That was how I learned that the world changes between heartbeats; that life is never an absolute, but always a wager.

I was allowed to see my father's body. Some kind soul had wrapped gauze around his head. He looked like he was asleep, but when I touched his hand, it was cold, like a marble bench in winter that you will not linger on, no matter how weary you might be. I thought of how his heart must have caught when he lost his footing. I wondered if the last thing he saw was his own sky.

Finn held my hand tight as I signed paperwork, blinked at questions about funeral homes, answered in a daze. Finally, a nurse gave me a plastic bag with the hospital logo on it. Inside was my father's wallet, his reading glasses, his wedding ring. Identity, insight, heart: the only things we leave behind.

In the taxi on the way home, Finn kept one arm anchored around me while I clutched the bag to my chest. I reached into my purse for my phone and scrolled to the last text my father had sent me, two days ago. *Are you busy?*

I had not answered. Because I *was* busy. Because I was going to his place for dinner that weekend. Because he often decided he wanted to chat in the middle of business hours, when I couldn't. Because there were any number of items on my to-do list that took precedence.

Because I never thought that I'd run out of time to respond. The story of our life was a run-on sentence, not a parenthetical.

Are you busy?

No, I typed in, and when I pushed send, I started sobbing.

Finn reached into his jacket, looking for a tissue, but he didn't have one. I scrabbled inside my own coat pocket and came up with the rectangular printout of the painting I had gone to pack up just that morning, a thousand years ago. I looked at the red circles and arrows meant to signify the marks and chips on the frame, the nick on the canvas, as if they meant anything.

As if we don't all have scars that can't be seen.

Dear Finn,

Well, it's still beautiful here, and I'm still the only tourist on this island. In the mornings, I go out for runs or hikes, but in the afternoon the whole place is locked down. Which feels redundant, when you're this isolated.

Sometimes I find myself eye to eye with a sea lion or sharing a bench with an iguana and I'm just blown away by the fact that I'm that close, and there's no wall or fence between us, and that I don't feel threatened. The fauna was here first, and in a way they still lord it over the humans who now share the space. I wonder what it would be

*like if I wasn't the only one marveling over them. I mean, the locals
are all used to it. I'm a one-woman audience.*

*The great-granddaughter of the woman who is renting me a room
speaks English. She's a teenager. Talking to her makes me feel less
lonely. I hope I do the same for her.*

*Every now and then I get a hiccup of cell service and one of your
emails arrives in my inbox. It feels like Christmas.*

Are you getting any of these postcards?

Love, Diana

The next morning, when Beatriz rounds the corner with her trash
bag—a one-girl recycling crew—I am sitting at the shoreline, making a drip castle.

From the corner of my eye, I see her, but I don't turn. I can feel her
watching me as I scoop up a handful of wet sand, and let it sift
through my fingers, creating a craggy turret.

"What are you doing?" she asks.

"What does it look like I'm doing?" I say.

"It doesn't even look like a castle," she scoffs.

I lean back. "You're right." I hold out my hand for her plastic bag.
"Do you mind?"

She hands it to me. Mixed in with the same plastic water bottles
from the Chinese fishing fleets are twist ties, burlap curled with seaweed, scraps of foil. There's a broken flip-flop, green plastic soda
bottles, red Solo cups. There's electric-blue netting from a bag of or-
anges, and a tongue of rubber tire. I pull all of these out and use them
to fashion flags on my castle turret, a moat, a drawbridge.

"That's trash," Beatriz says, but she sinks down cross-legged beside me.

I shrug. "One person's trash is another person's art. There's a Ko-
rean artist—Choi Jeong Hwa—who uses recycled waste for his in-
stallations. He made a massive fish puppet out of plastic bags . . . and

a whole building out of discarded doors. And there's a German guy, HA Schult, who makes life-size people entirely out of garbage."

"I've never heard of either of them," Beatriz says.

I take the thong off the flip-flop and create an archway. "How about Joan Miró?" I offer. "He spent the end of his life on Mallorca, and he'd walk the beach every morning like you, but he'd turn the trash he collected into sculptures."

"How do you even *know* this?" she asks.

"It's my job," I tell her. "Art."

"You mean, like, you paint?"

"Not anymore," I admit. "I work for an auction house. I help people sell their art collections."

Her face lights up. "You're the person who says *I have one dollar, one dollar, do I hear two . . .* "

I grin; she does a credible job of imitating an auctioneer. "I'm more behind the scenes. The auctioneers are kind of the rock stars of the industry." I watch Beatriz take a handful of tiny shells and line the moat with them. "There was this one British auctioneer we all had a crush on—Niles Barclay. During auctions, I was usually assigned to be on the phone with a collector who wasn't physically present and make bids on his or her behalf. But once, I was pulled to be Niles Barclay's assistant. I had to stand on the podium with him and mark down the sales price of the item on the information sheet when the bidding closed, and hand him the next information sheet to read out loud. Once, our hands touched when I was passing him the paper." I laugh. "He said, *Thank you, Donna,* in his amazing British accent, and even though he got my name wrong I thought: *Oh my God, close enough.*"

"You said you had a boyfriend," Beatriz says.

"I did. I do," I correct. "We gave each other one free pass. Mine was Niles Barclay; his was Jessica Alba. Neither one of us has cashed in on our pass." I look at her. "How about you?"

"How about me what?"

"Do you have a boyfriend?"

She flushes and shakes her head, patting the sand. "I mailed your postcard," she tells me.

"Thanks."

"I could stop by, if you want," Beatriz says. "Like, I could come to your place every now and then and pick them up, if you're sending any more."

I look at her, wondering if this is an offer of help, or a need for it. "That would be great," I say carefully.

For a few moments, we work in companionable silence, forming crenellated walkways and buttresses and outbuildings. As Beatriz stretches, reaching into the trash bag, her sleeve inches higher. It's been a few days now since I saw her cutting herself. The thin red lines are fading, like high-water marks from a flood that's receded.

"Why do you do it?" I ask softly.

I expect her to get up and run away, again. Instead, she digs a groove into the sand with her thumb. "Because it's the kind of hurt that makes sense," she says. She angles her body away from mine and busies herself by connecting some twist ties.

"Beatriz," I say, "if you want—"

"If I were making things from trash," she interrupts, shutting down the previous line of conversation, "I'd make something useful."

I look at her. *We're not done talking about the cutting*, I say with my eyes. But I keep my voice casual. "Like what?"

"A raft," she says. She sets a leaf on the water of the moat, which keeps seeping into the sand until one of us refills it.

"Where would you sail?"

"Anywhere," she says.

"Back to school?"

She shrugs.

"Most kids would be thrilled with an unscheduled break."

"I'm not like other kids," Beatriz replies. She adds a bit of yellow plastic hair to her twist tie creation, which is a stick figure with arms and legs. "Being here . . . feels like moving backward."

I know that feeling. I hate that feeling. But then again, these are circumstances beyond normal control. "Maybe . . . try to embrace that?"

She glances at me. "How long are *you* going to stay?"

what you wish for, I think. When you're stuck in heaven, it can feel like hell.

"As soon as I find out more, I'll tell you. Not that I know how," I mutter. "This whole situation is just insane. I'll keep sending postcards. Anyway. I thought you'd want to know." I stare at the receiver for another moment and then hang it up and afterward realize I hadn't said *I love you.*

When I step into Abuela's living room, Gabriel is sitting next to her on the couch. He stands when he sees me. "All good?"

"Voicemail," I say.

"You'll stay in the apartment, obviously," he says, as if he's trying to make up for his reaction when he first found me here.

"I don't have any money—" That jogs a new worry in my mind— as sick as I am of eating pasta, I don't even have enough cash to feed myself.

"And we'll make sure you have food," Gabriel says, reading my thoughts. He bends down and kisses Abuela on the cheek. "I don't want to leave Beatriz too long."

I follow him out the front door, onto the porch. When he jogs down the steps, headed toward my apartment in the rear, I call his name. He turns, looking up at me, impatient.

"Why are you doing this?" I ask.

"Doing what?"

"Being nice to me."

He grins, a streak of lightning. "I'll try to be more of a *cabrón*," he says, and when I blink, he translates. "Asshole."

"For real, though," I press.

Gabriel shrugs. "Before, you were a tourist," he says simply. "Now, you're one of us."

What I want to do: crawl underneath the covers of my bed, and pretend that when I wake up, I'll realize this was all just a nightmare. I will breeze down to the dock, board a ferry, and begin the first leg of my journey back to New York City.

What I do instead: accompany Gabriel and Beatriz to a swimming hole inland. Beatriz says that if I'm all by myself I will just wallow in my misery, and I cannot contradict her because it's the rationale for every outing I've dragged her on this past week—when *she* was the one who needed distraction. She is carrying a snorkel and mask looped onto her arm, and it bounces against her hip as we hike. "Where are we going?" I ask.

"We could tell you," Beatriz says, "but then we'd have to kill you."

"She's not entirely wrong," Gabriel adds. "Most of the island is closed because of the pandemic. If the park rangers find you, they'll *fine* you."

"Or take away your tour guide license," Beatriz tosses over her shoulder.

Gabriel's shoulders tense, then relax again. "Which I am not using anyway."

She turns on a heel, walking backward. "Are we or are we not going to a secret place you used to take clients?"

"We are going to a secret place I used to go to as a boy," he corrects.

We finally reach a brackish pond with water that is the color of rust and bordered by brush and thickets of fallen, twisted branches. As Isabela goes, it is far from the prettiest of landscapes. Beatriz begins to strip down to her bathing suit and long-sleeved rash guard, leaving the rest of her clothes in a pile. She fits her snorkel and mask to her face, then dives into the muddy lagoon.

"Maybe I'll just wait here," I say.

Gabriel turns in the act of pulling his shirt over his head and smiles. "Now who is judging a book by its cover?"

He kicks off his shoes and splashes into the water, and reluctantly I peel down to my bathing suit and wade in. The bottom drops away sharply, unexpectedly, and I find myself swallowed up by the water. Before I can even panic, a strong hand grabs my arm, holding me up as I sputter. "Okay?" Gabriel asks.

I nod, still choking a little. My fingers flex on his shoulder. This close, I realize that he has a freckle on his left earlobe. I look at the spikes of his eyelashes.

With a strong kick I free myself, and start swimming in the direction Beatriz went.

Gabriel overtakes me quickly; he is a stronger swimmer. He's headed straight for a wall of tangled mangrove roots, or so it seems, near which Beatriz's snorkel bobs. She lifts her face when we get closer, her eyes huge behind the plastic of the mask. The snorkel falls from her mouth as she scrambles up a makeshift ladder of roots and disappears into a fold in the brush. After a moment, her head sticks back out again. "Well?" she says. "Come on."

I try to follow, but my foot keeps slipping on the branches below the water. Gabriel's hands land square on my ass and he shoves, and I whip around fast with shock. He raises his brows, all innocence. "What?" he says. "It worked, yes?"

He's right; I have cleared the surface. I bang my knee and feel a scrape on the bare skin of my thigh but after a moment, I find myself on the other side of the mangrove thicket, staring at a twin lagoon. In this one, the water is almost magenta, and in the center a sandbar rises like an oasis. On it, a dozen flamingos stand folded like origami as they dip their heads into the pool to feed.

"This," Gabriel says from behind me, "is what I wanted you to see."

"It's amazing," I say. "I've never seen water this color."

"Artemia salina," Beatriz says. "It's a crustacean, a little shrimp, and it's what the flamingos eat that makes them pink. The concentration in the water makes it look so rosy. I learned that in class." At the mention of her studies, her face changes. The buoyancy of her shoulders seems to evaporate.

If I can't get off this island to go home, she also can't get off it to return to school.

She curls her fingers around the edges of her rash guard sleeves, pulling them more firmly down over her arms.

As if the mood is contagious, Gabriel's face shutters, too. *"Mijita,"* he says quietly.

Beatriz ignores him. She snaps on her snorkel, dives into the pink pool, and kicks as far away from us as she can, surfacing on the other side of the oasis.

"Don't take it personally," I say.

Gabriel sighs and rubs a hand through his wet hair. "I never know the right thing to say."

"I don't know if there's a *right thing*," I admit.

"Well, there's definitely a *wrong* thing," Gabriel replies, "and it's usually what comes out of my mouth."

"I haven't seen any new cuts," I tell him.

"I know she talks to you," he says, "and those conversations are for you to keep."

I nod, thinking of what Beatriz told me about her mother, and how that doesn't feel like a confidence I should break.

Gabriel takes a deep breath, as if he is gathering courage. "But will you tell me if she brings up suicide?"

"Oh my God, of course," I say in a rush. "But . . . I don't think that's why she cuts. I think for her . . . it's the exact opposite of being suicidal. It's to remind her that she's here."

He looks at me as if he is puzzling through my English. Then he tilts his head. "I'm glad you're staying," Gabriel says softly, "even if it is selfish of me."

I know he is speaking of whatever fragile thread I've spun between me and Beatriz, who clearly needs a confidante. But there is more to those words, a shadow crossing my senses. I feel my cheeks heating, and I quickly avert my face toward the flamingos. "What are those?" I ask, pointing to the small gray-and-white mottled birds that hop on the sand between the legs of the flamingos. "Finches?"

If Gabriel notices me trying to change the conversation with the finesse of a wrecking ball, he doesn't comment. "That's a mockingbird."

"Oh. And here I was, feeling Darwinian." I smile, trying for a joke.

Galápagos is, of course, famous for its finches—and for Charles Darwin. I'd read about him in every tour guide that was packed in my lost suitcase. In 1835, he came to the islands on the HMS *Beagle*, while just twenty-six and—surprisingly—a creationist who believed that all species were designed by God. Yet in the Galápagos, Darwin began to rethink how life had appeared here, on a spit of volcanic rocks. He'd assumed that the creatures had swum from South America. But then he began to realize that each island was vastly different geographically from the next, that conditions were largely inhospitable, and that new species popped up on different islands. By studying the variations in finches he developed his theory of natural selection: that species change to adapt to their circumstances—and that the adaptations which make life easier are the ones that stick.

"Everyone thinks Darwin based his work on the finches," Gabriel says, "but everyone's wrong."

I turn. "Don't tell my AP Bio teacher that."

"Your what?"

I wave my hand. "It's an American thing. Anyway, I was taught that finches look different on different islands. You know, like one has a long beak because on one island the grubs are deep inside a tree; and on another island, their wings are stronger because they have to fly to find food . . ."

"You're right about all that," he says. "But Darwin was a pretty shitty naturalist. He collected finches, but he didn't tag them all properly. However—likely by accident—he *did* tag all the mockingbirds correctly." He tosses a pebble, and a mockingbird takes to the air. "There are four different types of *los sinsontes* on Galápagos. Darwin collected them and measured their beaks and their sizes. When he got back to England, an ornithologist noticed that the mockingbirds were significantly diverse from island to island. The modifications that helped them adjust to the climate or terrain on a given island had been replicated, because the mockingbirds that had them were the ones who lived long enough to reproduce."

"Survival of the fittest," I confirm. We are sitting now on the edge of the sand oasis, watching flamingos tightrope-walk along the water. Beatriz is at the far end of the lagoon, diving and surfacing, over and over. Gabriel's lips move in silence, and I realize that he is counting the seconds she stays beneath the water.

"Do you ever wonder what animals we'll never know about?" I ask. "The ones that *didn't* make it?"

Gabriel's eyes stay on the surface of the water, until Beatriz appears again. "History is written by the winners," he says.

FIVE

The day after I learn that the island is not reopening, I walk into town to the bank, hoping to figure out a way to transfer money from my account in New York here. The bank is closed, but near the docks a bright collection of tables have been set up underneath a tent. Masked for safety, locals move up and down the aisles, picking up wares and chatting with each other. It looks like a flea market.

I hear my name, and I turn to see Abuela waving at me.

Although Abuela and I do not speak a common language, I've learned a few Spanish phrases, and the rest of our communication is still gestures and nods and smiles. She worked, I now know, at the hotel where I was going to stay, cleaning the rooms of guests. With the business closed, she is happy to cook and watch her telenovelas and take an unscheduled vacation.

She is standing behind a card table that has been draped with an embroidered cloth. On it are a few folded aprons, a box of some men's clothing, two pairs of shoes. There is also a cake pan and a small crate of vegetables and fruits like the ones Gabriel brought me. A word-search magazine is open in front of her, with a little sheaf of G2 postcards (does everyone have these?) stuck inside as a placeholder.

Abuela smiles widely and points to the folding lawn chair she has set up behind the table. "Oh, no," I say. "You sit!" But before she can respond, another woman approaches us. She picks up a pair of the shoes, looking at the tongue for the size, and through her mask asks Abuela a question.

They exchange a few more sentences, and then the woman sets on the table a large tote. Inside are jars of preserves, pickled garlic, red peppers. Abuela takes out one jar of jam and another of peppers. The woman slips the shoes into her tote and moves off to the next table.

I glance around and realize that although transactions are going on all around me under this tent, no one is exchanging money. The locals have figured out a barter system to combat their limited supply chain from the mainland. Abuela pats my arm, points to the chair, and then wanders down the aisle to survey the wares other locals have carted from home.

I can see double-jointed racks of used clothing, mud boots lined up in size order, kitchen utensils, paper goods. Some tables groan heavy with homemade bread or sweets, jars of beets and banana peppers. There are fresh cuts of lamb and plucked chickens. Sonny, from Sonny's Sunnies, has brought a full array of bathing suits and batteries and magazines and books. A fisherman with a cooler full of the catch of the day wraps up a fish in newspaper for a woman who hands him, in return, a bouquet of fresh herbs.

I could trade, too. But I don't have a surfeit of clothing or food I've grown or the ability to cook anything worth bartering for.

I run my hand back over my hair, smoothing my ponytail. I wonder what I could get for a scrunchie.

Just then, a zephyr of boys blows between the rows of tables. One small one straggles at the back, like the tail of a kite. He's red-faced and clearly trying to catch up to the bigger boys, the leader of whom is waving a battered comic book. As I watch, another boy sticks out his foot and trips the little one, who goes flying and lands headfirst under one of the tables. His crash stops the chase. Rolling onto his back, he sits up and shouts at the boy still holding the book. Even in Spanish, it's clear he has a lisp—which the bigger boy mocks. The bully rips the comic book in half and tosses it onto the smaller boy's chest before sauntering away.

The boy on the ground looks around to see who witnessed his humiliation. When his eye catches mine, I wave him closer.

Slowly, he walks toward me. He has dark brown skin and raven-wing hair that catches the sun. The mask he's wearing has the Green Lantern symbol on it. He clutches his torn comic book.

Impulsively I pull one of the G2 postcards from Abuela's maga-zine and root around for the pencil she was using to do the word searches. I flip the postcard to its empty side, and with quick, eco-nomical strokes, I begin to sketch the boy.

The summer between high school and college, I spent a month in Halifax, doing portraits of tourists in the Old City. I made enough money to stay at a hostel with my friends, and to spend the nights in bars. It was, I realize, the last time I traded in art of my own creation. After that, I spent every holiday building up my résumé for the in-ternship slot at Sotheby's.

Every artist has a starting point, and mine was always the eyes. If I could capture those, the rest would fall into place. So I look for the dots of light on his pupils; I draw in the flutter of lashes and straight slants of brow. After a moment, I pull at the strap of my mask, so that it swings free of my face, and then motion to him to do the same.

He's missing his front four teeth, so of course I draw that smile. And because confidence is a superpower, I give him a cape, like the hero in his torn comic book.

What feels rusty at first begins to flow. When I'm done, I pass the postcard to him, a mirror made of art.

Delighted, he runs the length of the tent, thrusting it toward a woman who must be his mother. I see some of the boys who'd been bullying him drift over, looking at what's in his hands.

I sit down, satisfied, and lean back in the lawn chair.

A moment later the boy returns. He is holding a fruit I've never seen before, the size of my fist, and armored with tiny spikes. Shyly, he sets it on the table in front of me and nods a thank-you, before darting back to his mother's table.

I scan the tent, searching for Abuela, and suddenly hear a small voice. *"Hola."*

The girl in front of me is thin as a bean, with dusty bare feet and braids in her hair. She holds out a dimpled green Galápagos orange.

"Oh," I say. "I don't have anything to trade."

She frowns, then pulls another postcard from Abuela's magazine. She holds it out to me, and tosses her braids over her shoulders, striking a pose.

Maybe I *do*.

When Abuela and I leave the *feria* two hours later, I am no richer in cash, but I have a straw sunhat, a pair of athletic shorts, and flip-flops. Abuela cooks me lunch: lamb chops, blue potatoes, and mint jelly that I received in return for my portraits. Dessert is the spiny fruit the boy gave me: guanábana.

Afterward, belly full, I leave Abuela's so I can take a nap at home. It is the first time, in my own mind, I've called it that.

To: DOToole@gmail.com
From: FColson@nyp.org

It's crazy—*everything's* been shut down. There are no flights out, and none in, and no one knows when that's gonna change. It's probably safer that way. Even if you could fly into the U.S., it's a shit-show. You'd probably have to quarantine somewhere for a couple of weeks, because we don't even have enough Covid tests right now for the people who are coming into the hospital with symptoms.

The truth is that even if you were home, I wouldn't be. Most of the residents who have families are staying at hotels, so they don't infect anyone accidentally. Even though I'm alone in the apartment, after I peel off my scrubs in the entry and stuff them in a laundry bag, the first thing I do is shower until my skin hurts.

You know Mrs. Riccio, in 3C? When I came home last night, I saw people I didn't recognize going in and out of her apartment. She died of Covid. The last interaction I had with her was five days ago, in the mailroom. She was a home health aide and she was terrified of catching it. The last thing I said to her was, Be careful out there.

One of my patients—she was extubated successfully but was in multiorgan failure and I knew she wasn't going to last the day—had a brief moment of consciousness when I went in to see her. I was in full PPE and she couldn't see my face well so she thought I was her son. She grabbed my hand and told me how proud she was of me. She asked if I'd hug her goodbye. And I did.

She was alone in her room and she was going to die that way. I was crying under my face shield and I thought: Well, if I catch it I catch it.

I know I took an oath. Do no harm and all that. But I don't remember saying I'd kill myself to do it.

Once we saw a movie, I don't remember the name, where there was a WWI soldier who was all of twenty, in a trench with a new recruit who was eighteen. The bullets were all around and the twenty-year-old was calmly smoking while the younger kid shook like a leaf. He asked, *How can you not be scared?* The older soldier said: *You don't have to be afraid of dying, when you're already dead.*

Whatever is going to happen is going to happen, I figure.

I read that the Empire State Building will be lit up red and white this week for healthcare workers. We don't give a fuck about the Empire State Building, or about people banging pots and pans at 7 P.M. Most of us won't ever see or hear it, because we're in the hospital trying to save people who can't be saved. What we want is for everyone to just wear a mask. But then there are people who say that requiring a mask is a gross infringement of their bodily rights. I don't know how to make it any more clear: you don't have any bodily rights when you're dead.

I'm sorry. You don't need to listen to me vent. But then again, this probably isn't even getting through to you.

Just in case it is: your mom's place keeps calling.

A few days later, while Beatriz is occupied making tortillas with her grandmother, I ask to borrow Abuela's phone to leave another message for Finn. Gabriel has taught me how to dial direct internationally, but calls are expensive, and I don't want Abuela to incur the costs, so I keep the conversation brief—just letting Finn know I'm all right, and I'm thinking of him. I save everything else for the postcards Beatriz mails.

Then I call my mother's memory care facility. Although I haven't received any emails or voicemail from them, that may be a function of the internet here, since Finn said they've left messages on our landline at the apartment. The last time The Greens reached out so doggedly, there was a glitch in the direct deposit that paid my mother's monthly room and board. The administration was all over it like white on rice, until I smoothed out the mistake and their money came through the wire. It will not be easy to sort out another bank error from a quarantined island.

I dial the number and a receptionist answers. "This is Diana O'Toole," I say. "Hannah O'Toole's daughter. You've been trying to reach me?"

"Hold please," I hear.

"Ms. O'Toole?" A new voice speaks a moment later. "This is Janice Fleisch, the director here—I'm glad you finally called back."

It feels pejorative, and I try not to get my hackles raised.

I look over at the counter, where Abuela is showing a recalcitrant Beatriz how to knead lard into flour to make dough. Curling the phone line around me, I turn, hunching my shoulders for privacy. "Is there a problem with my account? Because I'm not in New York at the—"

"No, no. Everything's fine there. It's just that . . . we've had an outbreak of Covid at our facility, and your mother is ill."

Everything inside me stills. My mother has been sick before, but it's never merited a call.

"Is she . . . does she need to go to the hospital?" Were they calling to get my permission?

"Your mother has a DNR," she reminds me, a delicate way of saying that no matter how bad it gets, she won't be given CPR or taken to the hospital for life-sustaining measures. "We have multiple residents who've contracted the virus, but I assure you we're doing everything we can to keep them comfortable. In the spirit of transparency we felt that you—"

"Can I see her?" I don't know what I could possibly do from here; but something tells me that if my mother is really, really sick, I will know by looking at her.

I think of Mrs. Riccio, in apartment 3C.

"We're not allowing visitors right now."

At that, a crazy laugh breaks out of me. As if I could even come. "I'm stuck, outside the country," I explain. "I barely have any phone service. There has to be something you can do. *Please.*"

There's a muffled sound, an exchange of words I can't hear. "If you call back this number, we'll get one of our aides to FaceTime with you," I hear, and I fumble around for a pen. Abuela has a marker attached to a whiteboard on her fridge; I grab it and write the digits down on the back of my hand.

When I hang up, my hand is shaking. I know that people who catch this virus do not always die. I also know that many do.

If my mother sees me on video, she might not even recognize me. She could get agitated, just by being forced to talk to someone she can't place.

But I also know I need to see her with my own eyes.

I am so focused on this, I forget I am in a place that lacks the technology to make this possible.

I hang up Abuela's phone and punch the new number into my cell, but there isn't a signal. "Dammit," I snap, and Abuela and Beatriz both look up. "I'm sorry," I mutter, and I dart out to the porch, holding my phone up in various directions as if I could attract connectivity like a magnet.

Nothing.

I smack my phone down beside me and press the heels of my hands to my eyes.

She has been an absent mother, and now I am an absent daughter. Is that quid pro quo? Do you owe someone only the care they provided for you? Or does believing that make you as culpable as they were?

If she dies, and I'm not there . . .

Well.

Then you won't be responsible for her anymore.

The thought, shameful and insidious, vibrates in my mind.

"Diana."

I look up to find Gabriel standing in front of me, holding a hammer. Has he been here the whole time? "My mother's sick," I blurt out.

"I'm sorry . . ."

"She has Covid."

He takes a step back involuntarily, and rubs his free hand across the nape of his neck.

"She's in an assisted living facility and I'm supposed to video-chat but my stupid phone still won't work here and—" I swipe at my eyes, frustrated and embarrassed. "This *sucks*. This just *sucks*."

"Try mine," he suggests. He pulls out his own phone, but it's not the device that's the problem. It's this whole damn island. While the local cellular network seems to function, anything that requires any real bandwidth is a complete loss.

Gabriel types something into his phone and then says, "Come with me." I fall into place beside him, but he is walking so fast I have to jog to keep up. He stops at the hotel I was supposed to stay at. Although I've tried to steal its Wi-Fi, as Beatriz suggested, the network hasn't shown up—likely because the business is shuttered. This time, however, Elena is standing outside the door, waiting with a ring of keys. "Elena," Gabriel says. *"Gracias por venir aquí."*

She dimples, combing her hands over the long tail of her braid. *"Cualquier cosa por ti, papi,"* she says.

I lean closer and murmur, "Do I want to know—"

"Nope," Gabriel cuts me off just as Elena loops her arm through his and presses herself up against him. She glances over her shoulder at me and whips her head back to Gabriel so fast her braid smacks against my arm.

Is a hotel with no guests even a hotel? The lobby feels small and stale, until Elena turns on the lights and an overhead fan. She boots up a modem behind the front desk, chattering to Gabriel in Spanish as we wait. She seems to be talking about her tan or a bra or something because she pulls aside the fabric and peers down at her bare shoulder, then sends a blistering smile toward him.

"Um," I say. "Is it ready?"

She glances at me like she's forgotten I'm here. When she nods, I find the network on my phone. I dial the memory care facility number I was given and wander off into a small room filled with tables, each wearing a bright cotton tablecloth.

When a face swims into view on my screen, I blink. The person on the other end is nothing more than a set of eyes above a mask, and that's behind a plastic face shield. She has a paper cap covering her hair, too. "It's Verna," the woman says, and she gives a little wave. I recognize her name; she is one of the aides who takes care of the residents there. "We were starting to wonder if you were ever going to call back."

"Technical difficulties," I say.

"Well, your mom's tired and she has a fever, but she's holding her own."

She holds up whatever device she's on and the view changes; from a distance I see my mother sitting on her couch with the television on, just like normal. My heart, which was racing, slows a little.

I let myself wonder, for the first time, what I was so afraid to see. Maybe vulnerability. My mother has been a gale force wind that blows in and out of my life before I can reorient myself. If she were still and silent in a bed, then I would know something is terribly wrong.

"Hi, Hannah," the aide says. "Can you look over here! Can you give me a little wave?"

My mother turns. She doesn't wave. "Did you take my camera?" she accuses.

"We'll find it later," Verna soothes, although I know my mother does not have a camera in her residence. "I have your daughter here. Can you say hello?"

"No time. We need to jump on the press convoy to the Kurdish village," my mother says. "If it leaves without us ..." She coughs. "Without ..." She dissolves into a fit of coughing, and the phone tumbles dizzily before coming to rest on a flat surface. The image goes black; I can still hear my mother hacking away. Then Verna's masked face reappears. "I have to settle her," she says, "but we're taking good care of her. Don't you worry."

The line goes dead.

I stare at the blank screen. There really isn't any way to tell if my mother's delirious, or if it is just her dementia.

Okay. Well. If she gets worse, they will call our apartment again. And if that happens, Finn will—somehow—update me.

Finn.

Immediately I try to video-chat him, too, making the most of the internet service. But it rings and rings and he doesn't pick up. I imagine him bent over a patient, feeling the buzzing in his pocket, unable to answer.

My mother has Covid, I type into a text. *So far she's stable.*

I tried to call you while I still had Wi-Fi but you were probably working. I wish you were here with me.

I tuck my phone into my pocket and make my way back to the front desk. Everything about Elena's body language suggests she is trying to pin Gabriel against any wall she can. Everything about Gabriel's body language resists it. When he sees me, relief washes over his features. "*Gracias,* Elena," he says. He leans in to give her a quick kiss on the cheek, but she turns at the last minute and presses her mouth against his.

"*Hasta luego,* Gabriel," she says.

As soon as we are out the door, he turns to me. "Your mother?"

"She's sick," I tell him. "She has a cough."

His brows pinch together, then smooth. "So, that's not too bad, right? I bet she was happy to see you."

She had no idea who I was. The words are on the tip of my tongue, but instead I ask, "Is Elena your ex?"

"Elena was one night of extremely poor decision making," Gabriel says. "I don't have very good luck with relationships."

"Well, I'm ninety-nine percent sure my boyfriend was going to propose to me here on our vacation, so there's that."

He winces. "You win."

"More like both of us lose," I correct.

Gabriel misses the turn to Abuela's, heading further into town toward the docks.

I say, "Far be it from me to tell you you're going the wrong way, but . . ."

"I know. I just thought . . . maybe you didn't want to spend today worrying about your mother." We stop on the pier, near a string of small pangas, the little metal boats fishermen use.

"What about Beatriz?"

"I already texted her. My grandmother is watching her." He shields his eyes, looking up at me. "I *did* promise I'd show you my island." He steps into a boat and holds out his hand so I can follow.

"Where are we going?"

"The lava *túneles*," Gabriel says. "They're on the western side of the island, about forty-five minutes out."

"We'll break curfew."

He scrabbles for a key under the plank seat and turns over the engine. Then he glances up, one side of his mouth quirked. "That's not all. Where we're going is closed even to locals," he says. "What is it you *americanos* say? Go big or go home."

I laugh. But I think: *I wish.*

Fishing, Gabriel tells me, is dangerous here.

He expertly moves the panga he has borrowed from a friend beneath delicate lava arches formed by volcanoes. We weave through the formations like thread through needles, the tide edging us precipitously close to the narrow walls of rock. Columns rise from the water, capped by land bridges with cacti and scrub growing over them. For some, the connector has already crumbled into the sea.

"Fishermen can catch bluefin tuna, *blanquillo,* cod, swordfish. But I had friends who headed out, and never came back," he says. "Riptides ... they're unpredictable. If your engine fails for some reason, you can get caught in one that moves three meters per second."

"So you mean ... they died?" I ask.

He nods. "Like I told you," he says. "Dangerous." He navigates through the steampunk maze of risen rock. "Look, over there, on the *aa* lava."

"The what?"

He points. "The spiky rock," he explains. "*Pahoehoe* lava is the other kind—the stuff that looks like it's melting." I follow his finger to see two blue-footed boobies. They face each other, bowing formally to the left and then to the right and back again, twin metronomes. Then they attack each other with their beaks in a frenzy of nips and clacks. "They're going to kill each other," I say.

"Actually, they're going to mate," Gabriel says.

"Not if he keeps *that* up," I murmur.

He laughs. "That guy's a pro. The older the bird, the bluer the feet. This isn't his first shoot-out."

It takes me a moment. "Rodeo," I correct, grinning. I watch him hop out of the boat and drag it onto the beach. "I know Beatriz learned in school, but how come you speak English so well?"

"I had to for my job," he says. He reaches under the seat again and tosses me a snorkel and mask. "You know how to use these, yes?"

I nod. "But I'm not wearing a bathing suit."

Gabriel shrugs, kicks off his flip-flops, and wades into the water fully dressed. It laps at his hips, his waist, and then he dives forward, surfacing with a shake of his shaggy hair. He fits his own snorkel and mask to his forehead. "Coward," he says, and he splashes me.

The water is a dizzy mirror of the sky, the sand like sugar under my feet. It feels strange having my shorts float around my legs and my shirt plastered to my body, but I get used to the sensation as I tread water. Gabriel dives a few feet away and a moment later I feel him tug at my ankle. *"Vamos,"* he says, and when he ducks beneath the surface this time, I follow.

The undersea world explodes with color and texture—bright anemone jewels, runnels of coral, wispy fronds of seagrass. For a little while we follow a sea lion that keeps playfully slapping Gabriel with its tail. Gabriel squeezes my hand, pointing out a sea turtle rhythmically sawing through the water. A moment later, in front of my mask floats a bright pink sea horse, a question mark with a trumpet nose and translucent skin.

Gabriel surfaces, pulling me with him. "Hold your breath," he says, and still grasping me, he kicks us powerfully to the seafloor, where a rocky promontory juts, polka-dotted with sea stars and a ripple of octopus. Gabriel twists until we are hovering in front of a small crevice in the boulder. Inside I see two small silver triangles. Eyes? I swim closer for a better look. But when I do, one moves, and I realize I am staring at the white-tipped fins of sleeping reef sharks.

I kick backward so fast that I create a wall of bubbles. Without looking to see if Gabriel is following, I swim as hard and as fast as I can back to shore. When I crawl onto the sand and rip off my snorkel, he's right behind me. "That was," I gasp, "a fucking *shark*."

"Not the kind that would kill you." He laughs. "I mean, maybe just a good bite."

"Jesus Christ," I say, and I flop onto my back on the sand.

A moment later, Gabriel sits down next to me. He is breathing hard, too. He pulls off his soaked shirt and throws it to the side in a soggy ball. When he lies back, the sun glints off the medallion he wears.

"What is that?" I ask. "Your necklace."

"Pirate treasure," he tells me.

When I look at him dubiously, he shrugs. "In the sixteen and seventeen hundreds, pirates used the canal between Isabela and Fernandina Island to hide from the Spaniards after raiding their galleons. Back then, this was a place where you could disappear."

Still, I think.

"The pirates knew the galleons went from Peru to Panama, and after they stole the gold, they hid it on Isabela." He raises a brow. "They also nearly hunted the land tortoise population to extinction, and they left behind donkeys, goats, and rats. But that wasn't nearly as interesting to a seven-year-old boy who was digging for buried treasure."

I come up on an elbow, invested.

"It was back in 1995 on Estero Beach—that's near El Muro de las Lágrimas. Two sailboats showed up, full of Frenchmen who were exploring Isabela, digging for treasure. I helped them for a few days—or at least I thought I did, I was probably more of a nuisance—and they found a chest. I helped them dig it out."

My eyes fall on his medallion. "And that was inside it?"

"I have no idea what was inside it." He laughs. "They took it away, still sealed. But they gave this to me as thanks. For all I know, it came from inside a cereal box."

I smack him on the shoulder. He grabs my hand to stop me from swatting him again, but he doesn't let go. Instead, he squeezes it, and looks me in the eye. "Speaking of thank-yous," Gabriel says, "Bea-triz—"

"Is a great kid," I interrupt.

He releases me, and seems to be carefully choosing his words. "When she would come home from school, there was always a wall between us. Every time I thought about knocking it down, every time I got close enough, I could feel so much heat on the other side—like a fire, you know. If you think there's a fire on the other side of a door, you don't rush in, because with even more oxygen, the flames are going to consume everything." He draws a line in the sand between us. "This past week, I don't feel as much heat."

"She's angry," I admit softly. "She was ripped out of her comfort zone. It's not fair, and it's not her fault. When you can't see light at the end of the tunnel, it's hard to remember to keep going."

"I know," Gabriel says. "I've tried to do things like this with her—distract her, you know, by taking her around the island? But she only goes through the motions, like it's a chore." He rubs his forehead. "For years, she lived with her mother, and God knows what Luz said about me. And then she was at school. And then when the virus hit, she called me, begging to come home."

Clearly, I misunderstood. "I thought she *had* to come home," I say.

"She's spent school vacations with her host family before—almost all of them," Gabriel says. "I don't know, maybe she was worried about the virus? Whatever it was, it was a gift. I was just happy she wanted to come back. I thought if we spent time together, she'd figure out that I wasn't actually a monster." He smiles a little. "I wish I could do what you do so easily."

"Talk to her?"

"Make her like me." He pulls a face. "That sounds pathetic."

I shake my head. "When you lose something that matters, you grieve," I say carefully. "Right now, Beatriz thinks she's lost her mom, her friends, her future." I hesitate. "So maybe there's a reason she keeps you at a distance. You can't grieve something if you don't let yourself get close enough to care."

His gaze snaps to mine—this seed of doubt is the absolution I can offer: the chance to think that Beatriz's aloofness might not be because she hates him, but the opposite.

Suddenly a marine iguana runs right between us, making me shriek and scurry backward. Gabriel laughs at me as the big lizard crawls with surprising speed into the water, bobbing a few times before it dives under the surface. "Why aren't those things as afraid of me as I am of them?" I mutter.

"They've had the run of the island longer than humans have," he says.

"Not surprising, since they look like baby dinosaurs."

"You should see the land iguanas in San Cristóbal. They turn turquoise and red during the mating season—we call them Christmas iguanas. That's how they get the ladies." He nods toward the water. "But the marine iguanas are my favorite."

I lie back down on the sand, looking up at the sky. "I can't imagine why."

"Well, they used to all be land iguanas. The ones that arrived came by accident ten million years ago, rafting in from South America on debris. But when they got here, there wasn't any vegetation. The only food was in the ocean. So their bodies changed, slowly, to make div-

what's in front of us. "Ten divers got spread out to the right of the cliff wall. But one, who wasn't quite as experienced at scuba, got sucked into the current to the left, and dragged down deep. My father, he pointed to the ten other divers and then he did this"—Gabriel touches his index fingers together—"he wanted me to stay close to them. I knew he was going to go after the other diver. I saw him swim into the current, and then when I couldn't see him anymore, I went after the others."

He shakes his head. "There was a clump of divers clinging to the rock face, together. After I got to them, I led them to the surface and set off a float so that the panga driver could get them. The boat was already a half mile north, picking up others who had surfaced a distance away. It went like that for a while—me treading water and trying to see the heads of the other divers and make sure the panga rounded them up. By the time that was done, I counted eleven divers and me, but my father and the last diver hadn't come up.

"We zoomed out to the left of the rock. I had binoculars, from the panga driver, and I was staring so hard at the surface of the water looking for a bobbing head or anything that moved, but the ocean . . ." Gabriel's voice caught. "It's just so goddamn big."

He fell silent, and I reached into his lap and squeezed his hand. I rested our fists on my knee.

"After an hour, I knew he couldn't have survived. At the depths he was at, he could have been dragged by the current a hundred feet or more. The percentage of oxygen in the tanks was meant for a shallow dive, and he knew going deeper would mess with his brain and his ability to function. He would only have had enough air for ten or fifteen minutes, that far down. Between swimming hard to catch up to the lost diver and inflating the diver's BC and unhooking his weight belt, my dad likely had even less time than that."

I think about my own father's death. I was not with him, and it happened too fast, but at the hospital, I was able to see his body. I remember holding his cold hand and not wanting to let it go, because I knew it would be the last time I ever got to touch him. "Did your father . . ." I start. "Did he ever . . ." But I can't seem to finish.

Gabriel shakes his head. "Bodies that drown in the ocean don't surface," he says quietly.

"I'm so sorry. What a terrible accident."

His gaze snaps up. "Accident? It was all my fault."

Dumbfounded, I stare at him. "How?"

"I was the one who tested the conditions. Clearly I got them wrong—"

"Or they changed—"

"Then I should have been the one to go after the diver," Gabriel insists. "So my father would still be alive."

And you wouldn't, I think.

He turns his head away from me. "I can't lead tours anymore, not without thinking about how bad I fucked up. I can't scuba-dive without thinking his body is going to drift in front of me. The reason I'm building the house and farming is because I have to be goddamn exhausted at the end of the day, or I have nightmares about what he must have been thinking in those last few minutes."

I'm quiet for a moment. "What he was thinking," I say finally, "is that his son would be safe."

Gabriel dashes a palm across his eyes, and I pretend not to notice. He stands up, using his weight to pull me to my feet. "We'd better get back," he says. "The return trip's not any shorter."

All around us, fumes rise from little pockets in the ground, as if we stand in a crucible. It is prehistoric and dystopian, but if you look closely, here and there are tiny green shoots and stalks. Something, growing out of nothing.

As we walk back across the fumaroles and the dark yawn of the caldera, Gabriel doesn't let go of my hand.

An hour later, the sun is skulking lower in the sky and we reach the crotched tree with the black lava rock where Gabriel left behind his heavier pack. We can see the huddled shape of it, propped against a tree, but there's another shadow as well, and as we get closer, it is clear that it's a person. I scramble in my pocket for the mask I haven't worn when it was just me and Gabriel, only to realize that it is Beatriz. She breaks into a run as soon as she sees us.

"You need to come *now*," she says, and she pushes a piece of paper into my hand.

It is an email, printed out on stationery from the hotel. *For immediate delivery to guest Diana O'Toole,* it reads. *From: The Greens. We have been trying to reach you. Please contact ASAP. Your mother is dying.*

On the way back to Gabriel's house, we sprint—and yet somehow, the distance seems even further than it did this morning. Distantly I hear Beatriz explain to Gabriel how the message arrived—something about Elena and an electrical short that caused a small fire in the hotel's utility room; how when she went to the hotel with her cousin so he could rewire and fix the circuits, and to make sure everything was in working order, she had powered up the front office computers and seen a series of emails, each more urgent, trying to get in touch with me. I hear Gabriel tell Beatriz to call Elena, to have the Wi-Fi up and running by the time we get there.

Still, it's two hours before we drop Beatriz at the farm and continue in Gabriel's rusty Jeep into Puerto Villamil, to the hotel. This time, there is no flirting from Elena. She meets us at the door, her eyes dark and concerned.

My phone buzzes, automatically connecting to the network. I ignore the flood of emails and texts bursting through this tiny crack in the dam of Isabela's radio silence. I pull up FaceTime, the last call I made to the memory care facility, and dial.

A different nurse answers this time, one I don't recognize. She is wearing a mask and a face shield. "I'm Hannah O'Toole's daughter," I say. All the breath seizes in my throat. "Is my mother . . . ?"

Those eyes soften. "I'll bring you in to her," the nurse says.

There's a lurching spin of scenery as whatever device she is holding is moved in transit. I close my eyes against a dizzy wave, expecting to see the familiar confines of my mother's apartment, but instead, the nurse's face appears again. "You should be prepared—she's decompensated very fast. She has pneumonia, brought on by Covid," the nurse says. "But at this point it's not just her lungs that are failing. Her kidneys, her heart . . ."

I swallow. It has been a couple of weeks since I saw her on video chat. I had used Abuela's phone to call The Greens twice. Just days ago, they told me she was stable. How could so much have gone wrong since then?

"Is she . . . awake?"

"No," the nurse says. "She's sedated heavily. But you can still talk to her. Hearing is the last sense to go." She pauses. "Now is the time to say your goodbyes."

A moment later, I am looking at a wraith in a hospital bed, the covers pulled up to her chin. She is hollow-cheeked, faded, taking tiny sips of air. I try to reconcile this image of my mother with the woman who hid in bunkers in active war zones, so that she could chronicle the terrible things humans do to each other.

Anger washes over me—why isn't anyone *doing* anything to help her? If she can't breathe, there are machines for that. If her heart stops—

If her heart stops, they will do nothing, because I signed a do not resuscitate order when she became a resident at The Greens. With dementia, there was no point in prolonging her life with any extenuating measures.

I am uncomfortably aware that the nurse is holding up the iPad or phone and waiting for me to speak. But what am I supposed to say to a woman who doesn't remember me now, and actively forgot about me in the past?

When she reappeared in my life, already in the throes of dementia, I convinced myself that putting my mother in a care facility was more compassionate than any consideration she'd ever given *me*. She couldn't move into my tiny apartment, nor would she have wanted to, when we were little more than strangers. Instead, I had figured out a way to use her own work to fund her living expenses; I had done the research and found the best memory care facility; I had gotten her settled and had patted myself on the back for my good deeds. I was so busy being self-congratulatory for being more of a daughter to her than she was a mother to me that I failed to see I had really just underscored the distance between us. I hadn't used the time to get to know her better, or to become someone she trusted. I had protected myself from being disappointed again by not cultivating our relationship.

Just like Beatriz, I think.

I clear my throat. "Mom," I say. "It's me, Diana." I hesitate and then add, "Your daughter."

I wait, but there is absolutely no indication she can hear me.

"I'm sorry I'm not there . . ."

Am I?

"I just want you to know . . ."

I swallow down the hurt that roars inside me, the wash of memories. I see my father hanging a giant map on the wall of my bedroom, helping me press thumbtacks into each of the countries where my mother was when she wasn't with us. I think of how, when her returns were inevitably delayed, he would distract me by letting me pick a color and then he'd cook entire meals in that monochrome. The heat of my blush at age thirteen when I had to explain to my father that I'd gotten my period. Scratchy phone connections where I pretended my mother was saying something other than *You know I'd be there for your birthday/recital/Christmas if I could.* Nights I'd lie in bed, ashamed for wanting her to just be my mother, when what she was doing was so much more important.

Feeling forgotten.

And in that second, staring through a screen at someone I never knew, I cannot trust myself to speak, because I'm afraid of what I might actually say.

You weren't there for me when it counted, either.

Quid pro quo.

Just then, the connection dies.

Elena tries rebooting the modem three times. One of those times, the video call is picked up, but the image freezes immediately and goes black. It is when Gabriel and I climb back into his Jeep and we are driving down the main street of Puerto Villamil with its tiny sliver of cell service that the text comes in.

Your mother passed tonight at 6:35. Our deepest condolences for your loss.

Gabriel glances toward me. "Is that—"

I nod.

"Can I do anything?" he asks.

I shake my head. "I just want to go home," I tell him.

He walks me to the door of the apartment, and I can see he is try- ing to find the words to ask if he should stay. Before he can, though, I thank him and tell him I just want to lie down. I wait until I hear his footsteps on the ceiling above, and I imagine him telling Abuela and Beatriz that my mother has died.

I hold my breath, waiting for the words to beat through my blood.

I pick up my phone and stare at the text from The Greens, and then swipe my thumb to delete it.

That's how easy it is to remove someone from your life.

I realize, even as I think it, that this is not necessarily true.

This is nothing like when I lost my father. Back then, it felt like a rip in the fabric of my world, and no matter how hard I tried, I couldn't hold the edges together. Even now, four years later, when I am going about my day, sometimes I brush up against that seam and it hurts like hell.

I find a bottle of caña in the cupboard—Gabriel gave me my own supply after our campout, along with a box full of fresh vegetables for meals this week. Since I don't have a shot glass, I pour a little into a juice cup, and then—shrugging—fill it to the top. I take a healthy swig, letting the fire run through me.

Right now, I just want to get fucking drunk.

I peel off my clothes, the ones in which I had hiked to the vol- cano (was that *today?*) and run the shower. Standing in the stream of water, needles pelting at my skin, I say the word out loud: *orphan*. I am nobody's child now. I'm an isolated island, just like the one I'm stuck on.

There are logistics that will have to be sorted out: burial, funeral, liquidating her apartment at the facility. Right now even thinking about it is exhausting.

I pull on clean underwear and one of Gabriel's old T-shirts, which hangs down to my thighs. I braid my hair to get it out of my face. Then I sit down at the table with the bottle of caña and pour my second full glass.

"Well, Mom," I say, tasting the bitterness of that title. "Here's to you." I take another gulp of the liquor.

By tomorrow, the media worldwide will be reporting on her death. The obituaries will be retrospectives of her career—from her first embedding in a war zone to the Pulitzer she won in 2008 for photos of a street demonstration in Myanmar that turned violent.

The award ceremony for that was held at a swanky luncheon in New York City in late May. My mother attended. My father did not.

He was in the bleachers at my high school graduation, cheering as I crossed the stage to get my diploma.

I put my head down on my crossed forearms and sift through my mind for one pure pearl of a memory of my mother. Surely there's one.

I discard one after another as they start off positive—a work trip I tagged along for; an image of her opening a Mother's Day gift I'd made in preschool; a moment where she stood in front of my canvas at a student exhibition and canted her head, absorbing it. But each of those recollections devolves quickly, pricked by a thorn of self-interest: a sightseeing promise broken when something came up; a phone call from her agent that interrupted the gift giving; a blunt and brutal criticism of proportion in my painting, instead of a crumb of praise.

Did you really hate me that much? I wonder.

But I already know the answer: *No.* To hate someone, you'd have to consider them worthy of notice.

Then something drips into my consciousness.

I am little, and my mother is putting film into her camera. It is a magical black box and I know I am not supposed to touch it, just like

I'm not supposed to go into her darkroom, with its nightmare glow and chemical scent. She balances the little machine on her knees and gently winds the slippery film until the teeth catch. It makes soft clicking noises.

Do you want to help? she asks.

My hands are tiny and clumsy, so she covers my fingers with her own, to circle the little lever until the film is taut. She closes the body of the camera, then lifts it and focuses on my face. She snaps a picture.

Here, she says. *You try.*

She helps me lift it and positions my finger on the shutter. I've seen her do it a thousand times. Except I don't know to frame the shot through the viewfinder. I don't really know what to look at, at all.

My mother is laughing as I push down on the shutter so hard it takes a flurry of photos, the sound like a pounding heart.

It occurs to me that I never saw those images. For all I know she developed them and got a crazy collage of blurry wall and ceiling and rug. Maybe I didn't capture her at all.

But maybe that doesn't really matter. For one second, it *had* been my turn.

New memories are sharp, and I wait for this one to draw blood. But ... nothing happens. If anything it's even more depressing to be sitting here half a world away, clinging to five seconds of motherhood, and wishing there had been more.

"Diana?"

I lift my head up from the table to find Gabriel standing in front of me. I blink at him as he turns on the light. I hadn't even noticed that it had gotten dark.

"I was headed back to the house," he says, "but wanted to see how you were."

"Still sober, that's how I am." I push the bottle across the table. "Join me." When he doesn't at first, I refill my glass. "I suppose you're going to tell me I shouldn't get wasted."

Gabriel takes a juice glass out of the cabinet and pours his own shot. He sits down across from me. "If ever there was a time to get wasted, it's when you're toasting someone you've loved and lost. I'm so sorry, Diana."

"I'm not," I whisper.

His gaze flies to mine.

"There," I say. "Now you know my terrible secret. I'm an awful, broken person. My mother died and I feel . . . nothing." I clink my glass to his. "*That* is why I'm drinking."

I gulp the alcohol, but it goes down wrong. Coughing and sputtering, I fold forward in the chair, trying—and failing—to catch my breath. It is like aspirating fire.

When I start to see stars at the edges of my vision, I feel a hand on the flat of my back, moving in circles. "Breathe," Gabriel soothes. "Easy."

My throat is burning and my eyes are streaming and I don't know if it's because I was choking or because I'm crying, and I'm not sure it matters.

Gabriel is crouched down next to me. He hands me a bandanna from his pocket so that I can wipe my face, but the tears don't stop. A moment later, with a soft curse, he wraps his arms around me. I sob into the curve of his neck.

I don't know when the air starts moving in and out of my lungs again, or when I stop crying. But I start noticing the rhythmic sweep of Gabriel's hand from the crown of my head to the tail of my braid. His lips against my temple. His breath falling in time to mine.

"You're not broken," Gabriel says. "You can feel."

When he kisses me, it feels like the most natural thing in the world. My fingers push through his hair as I fight to get closer. I'm struggling for breath again, but now I want to be.

Gabriel is still kneeling beside me. In one motion he picks me up and sets me on top of the table, standing between my legs. "I'm so glad I fixed this damn thing," he murmurs against my lips, and we both start to laugh. My hands slide up his forearms to his shoulders and my ankles hook behind his knees. He kisses like he is pouring himself into me. Like this is his last moment on earth, and he needs to leave his mark.

His palms move from my knees to my thighs, bunching the soft T-shirt. The whole time, we kiss. We kiss. When his fingers reach the elastic of my underwear, he stops and pulls back. He looks at me, his eyes so dark that I cannot see how far I've fallen. I nod, and he drags the T-shirt over my head. I feel his teeth scrape against my throat, against the chain of the miraculous medal, and then he paints words onto me with his tongue, moving between my breasts, down my belly, lower. *"Pienso en ti todo el tiempo,"* he says, hiking me to the edge of the table before kneeling again on the floor. His mouth is wet and hot through cotton. He feasts.

I am a lightning storm, gathering energy. I pull on Gabriel's hair, dragging him up, affixing myself to him like a second skin. The room spins as he picks me up and carries me into the bedroom, following me down onto the mattress in a tangle of limbs. He immediately rolls to his side so I don't bear his weight, and without him covering me I shiver beneath the ceiling fan. My hair has unraveled; he pushes it back from my face and waits. "Yes?" he asks.

"Yes," I say, and this time I crawl on top, pushing at Gabriel's clothes until they are gone; until I can sink onto him and into him and lose myself.

It isn't until afterward, when he has fallen asleep holding me tight, that I think maybe I've been found.

When I wake up, Gabriel is staring at me. I feel his hand flex on my shoulder, as if I am sand that might slip out of his grasp.

My head hurts and my mouth is dry but I know I cannot blame last night on the caña. I went into this with my mind clear, even if my heart was hurting.

Now, it's an anchor sinking in me.

Just one more second, I think.

I flatten my palm against Gabriel's warm chest, and I open my mouth to speak.

"Don't," he begs. "Not yet."

Because we both know what's coming. The slow untangling, the extraction. The excuses and the apologies and the veneer of friendship we will slap over this and never peek beneath.

He kisses me so sweetly, like it is a song in a different language. Even after he pulls back, I am still humming it. "Before you say anything," he begins.

But he doesn't finish. Because neither of us has heard the knock or the door opening, but we cannot miss the sound of breaking glass and china as Beatriz finds us knotted together, drops the breakfast she's kindly made me, and runs away.

By the time we have sorted out our clothes and hurried up to Abuela's, Beatriz is gone.

By unspoken agreement, I climb into Gabriel's Jeep with him. He is silent as he drives through town, scanning the empty streets for her. At the dock, he reverses direction, and heads for the highlands. "She could be back at the farm," he says, and I nod, because thinking of the alternative is too terrifying.

But I know that, like me, he saw the look on Beatriz's face. It wasn't just embarrassment at finding us. It was . . . betrayal. It was the expression of someone who realized she was well and truly alone.

It was a look I hadn't seen on her face since the very first time I saw her on the dock at Concha de Perla, watching her own blood drip from her fingertips.

In the time I'd been on Isabela, Beatriz had moved from desperation to resignation. If she hadn't been exactly joyous about this homecoming, at least now she seemed to be less tormented. She hadn't been cutting herself. Her old wounds were silver scars.

And now we'd ripped them open again.

I know that cutting does not always precede suicide. But I also know that sometimes, it does. Beatriz let her guard down with me; she trusted me to be her person. And then I gave myself to someone else.

A small sinkhole forms in me, filled with guilt. *Finn. My mother.* There is so much wrong with what I did last night. But I push all that out of my head because right now nothing matters but finding Beatriz and talking her down from her ledge.

A whisper in my bones: *Coward.*

"This is a small island," Gabriel says tightly. "Until it isn't."

I know what he means. There are endless trails and furrows through Isabela that aren't accessible by car; there are poisonous plants and spined cacti in some places and thick greenery you can't see through in others. There are countless ways you can hurt yourself—unintentionally, or on purpose.

"We'll find her," I tell him. I lift my hand, planning to cover his on the stick shift, but on second thought, put it back in my lap.

I stare out the passenger-side window, scanning every flutter of movement to see if it might be a girl on the run. There's no way she could have outpaced us on foot. But maybe she took a bicycle from Abuela's. Maybe she got a head start on us when we made a false start by turning toward town.

When we finally reach the farm, I open the Jeep's door before we even come to a complete stop. I run into Gabriel's house, yelling for Beatriz. He is on my heels, wildly looking around the living room and throwing open the door to her bedroom to find it empty.

I stand in the doorway as he sinks down onto the mattress. "Shit," he mutters.

"Maybe she just needs time alone," I say quietly, hopefully. "Maybe she's on her way back right now."

His haunted gaze meets mine, and I realize this is not the first time he's searched far and wide for someone he loved who'd gone missing.

Suddenly he grabs Beatriz's backpack from beside the bed and dumps the contents on the mattress.

"What are you looking for?" I ask.

"Something she took? Something she didn't?" He unzips an inner pocket and stuffs his hand inside. "I don't know."

A clue. A hint to where, on this island, she would have gone to disappear.

I open the top drawer of the bureau, letting my hand sift through panties and bras, when my fingers brush against something that feels like a diary.

I dig deeper into the recesses of the drawer. It's not a diary or a journal or a book at all. It's a stack of postcards, banded together with a hair elastic.

It's all of the postcards I wrote Finn. The ones that Beatriz told me she mailed.

I feel like I've been run through with a sword. I pull off the elastic and shuffle through the cards, all G2 TOURS on one side, and my cramped handwriting on the other. This was the one connection I had to Finn. Even if I couldn't reliably speak to him or get his emails, I was hopeful that he was hearing every now and then from me.

Except . . . he wasn't.

Finn is thousands of miles away, without any word from me. Given our last abortive phone call, he must assume I'm pissed at him. At the very least he'll think I've put him out of my mind.

I look at Gabriel and realize that, last night, this was true.

The contents of Beatriz's backpack—textbooks and a phone charger and earbuds and some granola bars—are littered around him. But Gabriel is holding a Polaroid and frowning slightly. A line of tape runs down the middle, carefully piecing together something that was previously sliced apart.

On one side of the photograph is a pretty girl, with corkscrews of blond hair. She has her arm around Beatriz, her other hand extended to take the photo. Their eyes are closed, as they kiss.

Ana Maria.

The expression on Beatriz's face is one I've never seen: pure joy.

"Who is this girl?" Gabriel murmurs.

I wonder what he is thinking. "Her host sister, a friend from Santa Cruz."

"A *friend*," he mutters, and at first I think he is reacting to Beatriz kissing a girl. But when he touches a fingertip to the Scotch tape down the center of the photograph, I realize he's angry at whoever broke Beatriz's heart so cleanly that she would tear apart this picture, and then regretfully patch it back together. "When her school closed, Beatriz begged to come back here. Is this why?"

I love that Gabriel has shoved aside the unimportant details—his daughter falling for a girl is inconsequential; what matters is that she was hurt. That she *still* is. That we are just the latest in a line of people she cared for who let her down.

I think of what Beatriz said to me when we were in the trillizos.

Truth or dare. Unconditional love is bullshit. She loved me, but not like that.

I wanted to know what it would be like to just let go.

"Gabriel," I breathe. "I think I know where she is."

The three volcanic tunnels are not that far from Gabriel's farm. We get as close as we can by truck and then Gabriel slings ropes and a rappelling harness over his shoulder. As we tramp through the thick ground cover, I call out Beatriz's name, but there is no answer.

I think about how far the ladder went into the shaft, how black it was below that. I wonder how much further she would have had to fall.

Curling my hand around Abuela's miraculous medal, I pray.

"Beatriz," I scream again.

The wind whispers through the brush and whips my hair around my face. Gabriel finds a sturdy tree and wraps one end of the rope around it, tying a series of impossible knots. It is an unfairly beautiful day, with puffy white clouds dancing across the sky and birdsong like a symphony. I stand in front of the three volcanic tunnels. If she's even here, she could be in any of them.

At the bottom of any of them.

"I'm going down," I tell Gabriel.

"What?" His head snaps up in the middle of securing the rope. "Diana, wait—"

But I can't. I start descending the ladder of the tunnel beside the one Beatriz and I climbed into, waiting for my eyes to adjust to the darkness. The distant sun bounces off minerals in the rock walls, glowing gold. I climb deeper, swallowed by this stone throat.

The only sound is the rhythmic drip of water on rock. *Plink. Plink.* And then a choked sob.

"Beatriz?" I cry, moving faster. "Gabriel!" I yell. "In here!" I lose my footing on the slick ladder in my hurry. "Hang on. I'm coming."

A beat, and then her voice threads toward me. "Just go away," Beatriz sobs.

Her words are disembodied, floating like ghosts. I can't see her anywhere below me. "I know you're upset about what you saw," I say, climbing down and down and down, until I reach the end of the ladder, and still she's not there. Wildly, I look between my feet on the bottom rung, wondering if I will see her broken body below me.

"I should never have talked to you," Beatriz says. I cannot see her; I go still and listen for the bounce of sound. I follow the soft hitch of her crying and—there—a shadow moving in a shadow. She clings to another ladder on the far side of the lava tube. There are a few straggling ropes left behind by others.

"I thought . . . you cared. I thought you meant what you said. But you're just like everyone else who says that and then leaves."

"You *do* matter to me, Beatriz," I say gently. "But I was always going to leave."

"Did you tell my dad that before or after you fucked him?"

I wince. "I didn't mean for that to happen."

"Yeah, sure. Keep digging that hole . . ."

"This isn't about him. This is about *you*," I say. "And I do care about you, Bea. I do."

Her sobs get louder. "Stop lying. Just fucking stop saying that."

The ladder shudders as booted feet strike the wall beside me. "She's not lying, Beatriz," Gabriel says, falling into view in the space between me and his daughter. He has the rappelling rope wrapped around him, a link to the world above. It is taut and seems too thin to support his weight. If it snaps, he is too far to grab either of the ladders Beatriz and I stand on. "When you care about someone, it just . . . happens," he says quietly. "None of us get to choose who we love."

I hold my breath. Is he talking about the two of us? About Beatriz and Ana Maria? About his ex?

As he is speaking, he has shifted his weight, canting his feet for balance on the slick wall. Incrementally, he's trying to make his way to Beatriz without startling her into doing something rash.

"You'd be better off without me," Beatriz sobs, the sentence torn from her throat. "Everyone else is."

Gabriel shakes his head. "You're not alone, even if you feel like you are. And I don't *want* to be alone." His breath catches. "I can't lose you, too."

He stretches out his hand toward her.

Beatriz doesn't move. "You don't even know who I really am," she says, her voice hushed in shame.

Their breathing circles, echoes.

"Yes I do," Gabriel says. "You're my baby. I don't care what else you are . . . or aren't. That's the only thing that matters."

His fingertips reach further through the void.

Beatriz meets him halfway. In the next moment, Gabriel has gathered her into his arms and lashed her tight against him with the ropes. He whispers to her in Spanish; she clings to his shoulders, drawing shuddering breaths.

Slowly, the three of us inch toward the light.

The next few hours pass in a blur. We take Beatriz down to Abuela's, because Gabriel doesn't want to leave her alone in the farmhouse while he ferries me back to the apartment. Abuela bursts into tears when she sees Beatriz and starts fussing over her. Beatriz is still weepy and silent and embarrassed, and Gabriel focuses all his attention and energy on her, as he should.

At some point, I slip out of Abuela's home and walk down to my basement apartment, sitting on the short retaining wall that separates it from the beach. With all the healing that has to happen in that family, I don't belong there.

But.

I'm starting to wonder where I *do* belong.

I think about the postcards in Beatriz's drawer that weren't sent. The things I wanted Finn to know. The things I will never tell him.

I don't know how long I sit on the little wall, but the sun staggers lower in the sky and the tide goes out, leaving a long line of treasure on the sand: sea stars and pearled shells and seaweed tangled like the hair of mermaids.

I can sense Gabriel walking up behind me even before he speaks. Space is different when he is in it. Charged, electrical. He stops just short of the spot where I sit, staring at the orange line of the horizon. I turn my chin, acknowledging him. "How is she?"

"Asleep," he says, and he steps forward. His hair is mussed by the breeze, as if it, too, sighs to see him.

He sits down next to me, one leg drawn up, his arm resting on his knee. "I thought you'd want to know she's all right," he says.

"I did," I tell him. "I do."

"We've been talking," Gabriel says hesitantly.

"About . . . school?" *About Ana Maria.*

"About all of it." He looks at me. "I'm going to stay with her to-night." A faint blush stripes his cheekbones. "I didn't want you to think that—"

"I wasn't expecting you to—"

"It's not that I don't—"

We both stop talking. "You're a good father, Gabriel," I say quietly. "You *do* protect the people you love. Don't second-guess that."

He takes the compliment awkwardly, his eyes sliding away from mine. "You know, I named her. Luz wanted something from a tele-novela she was obsessed with at the time—but I insisted on Beatriz. Maybe I knew what was coming."

"What do you mean?"

"Beatriz is the one who kept Dante going when he walked through hell. And every time I've found myself suffering, my Beatriz is the one who pulls me back."

This pushes on something so tender and bruised inside me, and instead of examining that reaction, I try to make light of it. "I'm shocked."

"That I named her Beatriz?"

"That you've read *The Divine Comedy*."

He smiles faintly. "There's so much about me you have yet to learn," he says, but there is a thread of sadness in the words, because we both know I never will.

He stands, blocking my view of the ocean. He holds my face in his palms and kisses my forehead. "Good night, Diana," Gabriel says, and he leaves me alone with the stars and the surf.

I pull the night around me like a coat. I think of New York City and Finn and my mother. Of commuter sneakers and Sunday brunch at our favorite café when Finn wasn't working and the blue Tiffany box hidden in the back of his underwear drawer. I think of the rush of relief when I manage to catch the subway car before it pulls out of the station and the taste of cheesecake I craved and bought at three A.M. and the hours I spent on Zillow dreaming of houses in Westchester we could not afford. I think of the smell of chestnuts from street vendors in the winter and asphalt sinking under my heels in the summer. I think of Manhattan—an island full of diverse, determined people hustling toward something better; a populace that doesn't sleepwalk through their days. But it all feels a lifetime away.

Then I think about *this* island, where there is nothing but time. Where change comes slowly, and inevitably.

Here, I can't lose myself in errands and work assignments; I can't disappear in a crowd. I am forced to walk instead of run, and as a result, I've seen things I would have sped past before—the fuss of a crab trading up for a new shell, the miracle of a sunrise, the garish burst of a cactus flower.

Busy is just a euphemism for being so focused on what you *don't* have that you never notice what you *do*.

It's a defense mechanism. Because if you stop hustling—if you pause—you start wondering why you ever thought you wanted all those things.

I can no longer tell the sky from the sea, but I can hear the waves. A loss of sight; a gain of insight.

When Finn and I booked a trip to the Galápagos, the travel agent told us it would be life-changing.

Little did she know.

To: DOToole@gmail.com
From: FColson@nyp.org

Whenever someone gets extubated in the Covid ICU, "Here Comes the Sun" plays on the loudspeakers. It's like in the Hunger Games movie, when someone dies, but the reverse. We all look up and stop what we're doing. But then again, days go by when we don't hear it at all.

Today, when I left the hospital for the first time in 36 hours, there was a refrigerated truck parked outside for the bodies we can't stuff into the morgue.

I bet every single one of those people came into the ER, think-ing: it will only be a day or two.

I do not see Beatriz or Gabriel for five days. Even Abuela seems to be missing, and I assume that they are all up at the farmhouse to-gether. I convince myself very easily that the reason I feel relieved has everything to do with Beatriz getting help and nothing to do with me being able to avoid Gabriel. The truth is, I don't know what to say to him. *This was a mistake* is what sits bitter on my tongue, but I'm not sure what it refers to: the night with Gabriel, or all the years that led up to it.

So every time I leave my apartment and do not see him, it is a reprieve. If I don't see him I can pretend it didn't happen, and post-pone grappling with the consequences.

One day, I hiked to the Wall of Tears, hoping to find another mira-cle of cell service. When those bars appeared on my phone, I called The Greens first, arranging for my mother's cremation and explaining that

I was still stuck outside the country. Then I called Finn, only to be put through directly to his voicemail. *It's me*, I said. *I wrote you postcards, but they . . . didn't make it there. I just wanted to let you know I'm thinking of you.* And then I didn't trust myself to say anything else.

On another sunny, perfect day on Isabela, I pull on my bathing suit, take the snorkel and mask from Gabriel's apartment, and walk through the streets of Puerto Villamil, headed to Concha de Perla one more time. A couple of storekeepers—who, like everyone else, have become less strict with the rule about curfew—recognize me and wave, or call out hellos through their masks. A few have come up to me at the feria, trading me sunblock and cereal and fresh tortillas for portraits that they then hang in their establishments.

When I get to the dock at Concha de Perla, there is a massive sea lion lolling on one of the benches. It raises its head at my approach, twitches its whiskers, and then flings itself back into its nap. I strip to my bathing suit and walk down the stairway into the ocean, fitting the mask to my face and swimming with strong strokes into the heart of the lagoon.

A huge, dark shape rises in my peripheral vision. I turn to see a giant marble stingray moving in tandem with me. Its wings ruffle past, a hem sweeping the dance floor. It brushes my fingers gently, deliberately, as if to convince me there's no threat. It feels like stroking the soft, wet velvet underskirt of a mushroom.

Six weeks ago this would have sent me into a conniption. Now, it's just another living creature sharing space with me. I smile, watching it veer away from me underwater, until it becomes a dot in the deep blue field and then vanishes.

I float on my back for a while, feeling the sun warm my face, and then lazily breaststroke back toward the dock.

Once again, Beatriz is sitting on it.

She isn't wearing her ubiquitous sweatshirt. Her arms are bare, crossed with silver lines. She hugs her knees to her chest as I climb the stairs, drop my mask and snorkel, and wring my ponytail dry. I sink down beside her. "Are you okay?" I ask quietly, the same words I first spoke to her on Isabela, a bookend.

"Yeah," she says, and she looks into her lap.

We fall into a strained silence. Of all the time I've spent with Beatriz, we've never had nothing to say.

"What you saw . . . with me and your father . . ." I shake my head. "You know I have someone waiting at home for me. It shouldn't have happened. I'm sorry."

Beatriz rubs her thumbnail along a groove in the wood. "I'm sorry, too. About not sending your postcards."

I've thought a lot about what might have made her lie to me about mailing them. I don't think it was malicious . . . more like she wanted to keep me to herself, once she'd made me a confidante. All the more reason, of course, that she would have been shocked to find me in bed with her father.

She trusted me. Just like Finn had trusted me.

Suddenly I feel like I'm going to be sick. Because as much as I don't want to face Gabriel to discuss what happened between us, I want even less to confess to Finn.

Beatriz looks at me. "I talked to my dad about Ana Maria."

"How'd that go?"

"Not as bad as I made it out in my head to be," she says ruefully.

"The mind is an amazing thing," I reply.

She considers this. "Well, it's not like I didn't have a good reason to worry," she adds. "There are a lot of people in the world who'd hate me because I . . . like girls. But my father isn't one of them." Beatriz ducks her chin. "I kind of feel bad for Ana Maria. She doesn't have parents like him, so she has to pretend all the time. Even to herself."

I don't know what to say to her. She's right. The world can be a fucked-up place, and I suppose you're never too young to learn that.

"I'm not going to go back to school," Beatriz tells me. "My father said he'll let me do online courses here. But I had to promise to talk to a therapist, in return. We Zoomed for the first time, yesterday." She grimaces. "Something else that wasn't as bad as I thought it would be."

"*Online* school?" I repeat. "And *Zoom*?"

"My dad paid Elena to open the stupid hotel and turn on the Wi-Fi so I could get a decent signal," Beatriz explains.

I raise an eyebrow. "What's he paying her with?"

Beatriz cracks a smile, and then I do, too, and we both laugh. I put my arm around her, and she lays her head on my shoulder. We watch a sea lion playing in the distance.

"You know," Beatriz says, "you could stay. With us."

I feel myself soften against her. "I have to go back to real life sometime."

She pulls away, a wistful expression on her face. "For a while," she says, "didn't this feel real?"

Dear Finn,

It's possible you won't get this postcard until I come home and hand it to you myself. But there are things I need to say, and it can't wait.

I've been thinking a lot about the things we do that are simply unforgivable. Like me not being with my mother when she died, or my mother not being around when I was growing up. Leaving you alone during a pandemic. You encouraging me to go.

I've thought a lot about that last one. When you told me you were trying to keep me safe . . . you might just have been convincing yourself it was the smartest course of action. Did you really not think I could manage to stay healthy? Did you actually believe that when the world is falling to pieces, it's better to be apart from the person you love, instead of together?

I am overthinking this, of course, but these days I have a lot of time to think. And I can't even blame you. I've said and done things, too, that I shouldn't have.

I know everyone makes mistakes—but until recently I have held everyone to a standard where making mistakes is a weakness. Me included—I haven't given myself the grace to screw up, to do better next time. It is exhausting, trying to never step off the path, worrying that if I do, I'll never get back on track.

So here is what I've learned: if, in hindsight, you realize you've messed up—if you have done the unforgivable—that does not mean that the terrible thing wasn't meant to happen. Sure, we may wish otherwise, but when things don't happen according to plan, it may be be-

It strikes me that Covid isn't the only thing that can take your breath away.

I remember the first time I saw Finn in a suit instead of scrubs—on an official date, waiting for me at a table at an Italian place in the Village. When I came in, late because of subway delays, he stood up and the room narrowed to the size of just us. I had to actively remember to draw in air.

A week later, in the middle of a heated kiss, his fingers found the strip of skin between my sweater and my jeans. It was like being branded, and all the breath rushed out of me in a sigh.

Months into our relationship as I reached for him in the dark, I remember thinking how lovely it was to have a body you knew as well as your own. How he gasped when I touched him the way he liked; how *I* gasped at the miracle of knowing exactly what that was.

Suddenly I realize how lucky I've been to have had Finn with me when I got sick. If he hadn't realized that I passed out from a lack of oxygen; if he hadn't gotten me to the hospital—well, I might not be sitting here now. "Thank you," I say, my voice thick. "For saving me."

He shakes his head. "You did that yourself."

"I don't remember any of it," I tell him. "I don't even remember being in the hospital before going on the vent."

"That's normal," Finn says. "And that's what I'm here for." The corners of his eyes crinkle, and I think that of all the horrible things about the masks everyone has to wear, this must be the worst: it is so hard to tell when someone is smiling at us. "I'll be your memory," he promises.

A part of me wonders how his recollection could be any less faulty than mine. For one thing, he wasn't here the whole time. And, in my mind, neither was I.

There are experiences our brains probably forget on purpose, so we don't have to suffer through them again. But there are experiences our brains remember that serve as some kind of red flag or warning: *Don't touch that stove. Don't eat that rotten food.*

Don't leave your boyfriend in the middle of a pandemic.

"The last thing I remember is you telling me I should go on vacation without you," I say quietly.

He closes his eyes for a moment. "Great. That's the part I was hoping you *wouldn't*," Finn admits. "You were pretty pissed at me for saying that."

"I . . . was?"

"Uh, yeah. You asked how I could even suggest that, if I really believed things were going to get so bad here."

In other words, everything I had felt in the Galápagos.

"You said clearly we had very different interpretations of a relationship. You kept talking about *Romeo and Juliet* and how if Romeo had just stayed in Verona, all the rest of the bullshit wouldn't have happened." He looks at me, confused. "I had no idea what you were talking about. I've never read it."

"You've *never* read *Romeo and Juliet*?"

Finn winces. "You said that, too." He looks at me. "You accused me of caring more about the money we were going to lose on the vacation and less about you. You said if I really loved you, I wouldn't let you out of my sight when all hell was breaking loose. The truth is, I made a mistake. I spoke without really thinking it through. I was tired, Di. And scared about working here, and taking care of patients who had the virus, and—" His voice breaks, and he bows his head. To my shock, I see that he's crying.

"Finn?" I whisper.

Those beautiful blue eyes, the color of his scrubs, the color of the sea in a country I never flew to, meet mine. "And I'm probably the one who brought it home to you," he forces out. "I'm the reason you got sick."

"No," I say. "That's not true—"

"It is. We don't know a lot, but it's pretty clear some people are carriers and they never show symptoms. I work in a *hospital*." He spits out that last word, and I realize he is nearly bowed over with the guilt he's been carrying. "I almost killed you," Finn whispers.

"You don't know that," I say, squeezing his hand. "I could have caught this at work or on the subway—"

He shakes his head, still steeped in remorse. "I was so tired that night that I didn't want to fight anymore. I didn't try to stop you when you went to bed early, and you were already asleep when I turned in for the night. When you woke up in the middle of the night to get some Tylenol I heard you and I pretended to be asleep, because I was afraid to pick up where we left off. And then the next morning, when I wanted to apologize, I could barely wake you up." He turns away, wiping his eyes with the shoulder of his scrubs.

Other things that leave you breathless: love so big that it tumbles you like a wave.

"I almost lost you. If I ever needed a lesson that saying goodbye isn't something you do casually, I sure as hell got one." Finn brings my hand to his cheek, laying my palm along it, leaning into my touch. "I will never ask you to go anywhere without me again," he says softly. "If you swear to me you'll never leave."

I close my eyes and see two blue-footed boobies, bobbing and weaving in an ancient dance, then snapping at each other's beaks.

They're going to kill each other.

Actually, they're going to mate.

My eyes fly open, my gaze fixes on Finn. "I promise," I say.

The intensivist comes to see me. His name is Dr. Sturgis, and Finn doesn't know him very well; he only started in the ICU at New York–Presbyterian at Christmas. He runs down my list of medications; he says my oxygen levels are improving. He asks me if I have any questions.

I am careful not to talk to Betty or Syreta about my memories of the Galápagos, because the response always involves Xanax or Ativan, and I don't want any more pharmacological interference in my mind. But contrary to what they've said in passing about how the hallucinations patients have on ventilators fade away, mine have not. If anything, they've been honed sharper and more brilliant, because I revisit them when I am alone in my room for hours on end.

"The ... dreams," I say to the intensivist. "The ones I had while I

was on the ventilator. They aren't like any other dreams I've ever had."
I force myself to continue; this is a physician, he can't dismiss my
concerns as foolish. "I'm having a hard time believing they're not
real."

He nods, as if he's heard this before. "You're worried about your
mental state."

"Yes," I admit.

"Well. I can tell you there's a physical explanation for anything
that doesn't make sense. When you're not oxygenating right, your
mental status changes. You have trouble interpreting what's actually
happening to you. Add to that pain meds and very deep sedation—
it's a recipe for all kinds of delirium. There are even some scientists
who think that the pineal gland, under stress, produces DMT—"

"I don't know what that is."

"It's the main ingredient in ayahuasca," Dr. Sturgis says, "which is
a psychedelic drug. But that's still just a theory. The truth is, we don't
really know what happens when we medically sedate someone, and
how your mind syncs your reality with your unconscious. For exam-
ple, at some point, you were likely restrained—most of the Covid
patients on vents try to rip out their IVs otherwise. Your brain, in its
drugged state, tried to make sense of the insensible, and maybe you
hallucinated a scenario in which you were tied down."

What I hallucinated wasn't confinement, but freedom. Now that
I'm constrained again it chafes. I want to wander to Sierra Negra. I
can still smell the sulfur. I can feel Gabriel's hand on my bare skin.

"Neurons fire and rewire during a near-death experience," the
doctor says. "But I can promise you, it was just a dream. A particu-
larly three-dimensional one, but still a dream." He looks down at my
chart. "Now, your nurse says you're having trouble sleeping?"

I wonder why everyone's answer involves more medication. This
will be Tylenol PM or zolpidem or something that will knock me
out. But that's not what I want. It's not that I can't sleep; it's that I
don't *want* to.

"Is it because you're worried about having more hallucinations?"
Dr. Sturgis asks.

After a moment, I nod. I can't admit the truth: I'm not afraid of revisiting that other world.

I'm afraid that if I return there, I won't want to come back.

I am moved to a step-down unit that isn't the ICU, which means I no longer have Syreta or Betty or the Hot CNA taking care of me. Instead, I am now in the ward I was in when I was first brought to the hospital, the one I don't remember. The nurses here are flat out, with more patients to attend to. It is impossible for Finn to sneak in to visit me here, because he's stationed in the Covid ICU and he's not allowed elsewhere due to safety protocols.

If anything, I feel even more isolated.

There are a *lot* of codes on this floor.

I realize that the vast majority of patients who move from this space to the ICU do not return. That I am the anomaly.

When a speech therapist comes in to see me, I am so grateful to interact with someone that I don't want to tell her I can already talk—even if it's raspy. Sara reads my mind, though, and says, "Speech therapy isn't just about talking. You're getting a swallow test. We'll try different consistencies of food to make sure you don't aspirate. If you pass, you get to have your NG tube removed."

"You had me at *food,*" I answer.

By now, I can sit up for nearly a half hour without getting dizzy, which is what makes me eligible for this swallow test. I dutifully sit with my legs swung over the side of the bed. Sara scoops some ice chips onto a spoon and places them on my tongue. "All you have to do," she says, "is swallow."

It's hard to do on command, but it almost doesn't matter, because the ice melts in the heat of my mouth and drips blissfully down, quenching my raw throat. As I do it, Sara holds a stethoscope up to my throat and listens. "Can I have more?" I ask.

"Patience, young grasshopper," Sara says, and I give her a blank look. "You millennials," she sighs, and she holds a cup with a straw to my lips. I suck up a mouthful of water, which is just as satisfying.

By the time we move on to applesauce, I am in heaven. When Sara moves to take the little dish from me I curl around it, hoarding, and hurriedly scoop another spoonful into my mouth.

I graduate to a graham cracker, which requires chewing—muscles that my jaw has to actively remember how to use. Sara watches my throat work. "Good job," she says.

I wait until I am sure no crumbs remain. "It's so weird," I muse. "To have forgotten how to eat."

She resettles the oxygen cannula into my nostrils as I lean back in bed again. "You'll have plenty more practice. I'm going to give the green light for the feeding tube to be removed. Tomorrow, you get to eat a whole meal while I watch."

A half hour later, a nurse I haven't seen before comes in to remove the nasogastric tube. "I cannot tell you," he says as he works quickly and efficiently, "how glad I am to see you again."

I try to read the name on the badge clipped onto his lanyard. "Zach?" I ask. "Did you take care of me before?"

He holds a hand to his heart. "You don't remember me. I'm crushed." My eyes fly to his, but they're dancing. "I'm *kidding*. But clearly, I'm going to have to up my game."

I rub the bridge of my nose, itchy without the tape adhering the feeding tube. "I don't . . . I don't remember being in this ward."

"Totally normal," Zach assures me. "Your O-two levels were so low you kept passing out. I'd be surprised if you *did* remember."

I watch him briskly wash his hands in the sink and towel-dry before snapping on a new pair of gloves. He seems competent and kind, and he holds a part of my history I may never recover. "Zach?" I ask quietly. "Would it be a surprise if I remembered things . . . that didn't happen?"

His eyes soften. "Hallucinations aren't uncommon for people who are sick enough to be in an ICU," he says. "From what I've heard, Covid patients are even more likely to have them, between the lack of oxygen and the deep sedation and the isolation."

"What you've heard," I repeat. "What else have you heard?"

He hesitates. "I'll be honest, you're only the second patient I've had who has gone to the ICU and survived to talk about it. But the other one was a man who was absolutely convinced that the roof of the hospital opened up like the Superdome, and twice a day light would shoot out of it, and one lucky person would be chosen to be lowered from a crane into that beam of light and get instantly healthy."

I probe the corners of my mind for hallucinations that are hospital-based, like this, but cannot find any.

"I was in the Galápagos," I say softly. "I lived on the beach and made friends with local residents and swam with sea lions and picked fruit right off the trees."

"That sounds like an awesome dream."

"It was," I say. "But it wasn't like a dream. Not like anything I've ever dreamed when I'm asleep anyway. This was so detailed and so real that if you put me on the island, I bet I could find my way around." I hesitate. "I can see the people I met like they're standing in front of me."

I watch something change in his eyes, as he puts on his professional regard. "Are you still seeing them now?" Zach asks evenly.

"You don't believe it was real," I say, disappointed.

"I believe *you* believe it was real," he says, which isn't an answer at all.

Although I am still testing Covid-positive—which Finn assures me is normal—he lobbies to get me out of the step-down Covid ward as fast as possible, because if you're in the hospital long enough you wind up getting sick with something else—a UTI, hospital-acquired pneumonia, *C. diff.* I feel ridiculous being in a rehabilitation unit when I'm not even thirty, but I also realize that there's no way I'm ready to go home yet. I still haven't managed to do more than sit upright in a chair, and even that took Prisha and a Hoyer lift for the transfer. I can't get myself to the bathroom.

To qualify for rehab, you have to be able to tolerate three hours of therapy a day. Some of it is physical therapy, some occupational, and for those who need it, speech therapy. The silver lining is that I will see people again. The therapists are completely covered in PPE to keep them safe, but at least three times a day I will have company.

And the more time I spend with people, the less time I spend replaying my memories of Isabela.

I am moved into a small room with a private bathroom, and I haven't been there for more than a half hour when the door opens and a tiny hurricane with red hair and snapping blue eyes blusters in. "I'm Maggie," she announces. "I'm your physical therapist."

"What happened to Prisha?" I ask.

"She doesn't leave the hospital; I don't leave the rehab unit. It's theoretically a single building, but it is like there's a special force field between us." She grins; there is a sweet gap between her front teeth. "Big Star Wars fan here. You watch *The Mandalorian*?"

"Um, no?"

"The guy's hotter with his helmet on," she says. She has approached the bed and already has stripped back the covers; her hands are firm and strong on my feet as she rotates my ankles. "My kids got me into that show. I have three. One came back home from college because of Covid. I can't believe it. He's a freshman; I thought I'd just gotten rid of him." She says this with another smile as she moves to my arms, pulling them over my head. "You got kids?"

"Me? No."

"Significant other?"

I nod. "My boyfriend is a surgeon at the hospital."

She raises her eyebrows. "Ooh, better be on my best behavior," she says, and then she laughs. "I'm just kidding. I'm gonna put you through the paces like I do everyone else."

As she moves my limbs as if I'm a rag doll (which, to be fair, I might as well be), I learn that she lives on Staten Island with her husband, who is a policeman in Manhattan, plus her displaced college student, as well as a seventh grader who wanted to be a nun last week but has, as of Tuesday, decided to convert to Buddhism, and a ten-year-old boy who will grow up to be either the next Elon Musk or the Unabomber. Maggie says she's already had Covid, which she's

"If I just beat this motherfucker," I say, "my veins must be full of antibodies." I flex my arm. "I'm basically a superhero."

That, finally, makes him smile. "Okay, Wonder Woman."

I lean a little closer. "I wonder if antibodies are contagious."

"I can categorically tell you they're not," Finn says.

"I mean, just in case," I murmur against his neck. "Maybe we should try to get some into you." I loop my arms around his neck and press my mouth against his. Finn hesitates, then kisses me back. I slide my hands under his sweater, feeling his heart beat against my palm.

"Diana," he breathes, a little desperate. "You just got out of rehab."

"Exactly," I say.

I don't know how to explain to him that when you find out you nearly died, there is a crucial need—a compulsion, really—to make sure you're alive. I need to feel healthy and vital and desired. I need to burn with something that is not fever.

"Let me show you what I've learned," I say to Finn, and I pull my sweatshirt over my head. I shimmy my leggings down to my ankles and kick them off. "And watch this." I get to my feet, turn to face him, and sit down on his lap with my knees on either side of him. "Stand, pivot, transfer," I whisper.

Finn's arms come around me as I grind against him. It is a matter of moments before his clothes are off, before the feel of his skin against mine sets me on fire. Teeth and lips and fingertips, my nails on his scalp, his palms bracketing my hips. I sink onto Finn and he flips us so that I am lying on the couch, dissolving around him. I succumb to the here and the now, focusing on the symphony of our breath, the percussion of our bodies, the crescendo.

When the buzzer rings, we are both so surprised we roll onto the floor.

"Shit," Finn says. "Dinner."

He scrambles to his feet and I am jealous of his easy, unthinking movement. In his hurry, he pulls on my sweatshirt instead of his own, and it stretches too tight across his chest. As Finn hops into his boxers, I watch. "Don't forget the . . . tip," I say.

A laugh bursts out of him. "I *cannot* believe you said that."

He is back a few minutes later, holding a brown paper bag full of Thai food. He looks at me, almost shyly. "Hungry?"

"Starving," I say.

I watch him put the food on the counter, take out some disinfectant spray and paper towels, and start wiping everything down. "What . . . what are you doing that for?"

He blinks at me. "Oh, right. You don't know. It's for safety. You should use gloves, too, when you go to the mailbox, and let the mail sit for two days, just to make sure—"

"To make sure of what?"

"That there's no virus on it."

He washes his hands again vigorously as I stand up and walk toward him. "You know what has no virus on it?" I ask, and I pull his head back down to mine.

The food cools on the counter as we tangle ourselves on the couch. When I finally unspool in Finn's arms, I open my eyes to find him watching me. He brushes my hair off my face. "Something's different about you," he murmurs.

"I like being back here," I whisper.

What he likely thinks I mean: *not in the hospital.*

What I actually mean: *not wandering in my clouded, confused thoughts. In his embrace and wholly, blissfully present.*

Finn is, and always has been, my anchor.

We eat in our underwear, and make love again, knocking over the sanitized cartons of food. At some point, we stumble to the bedroom and crawl under the covers. Finn's arm comes around me, holding my back tight against his front. It's not the way we usually sleep—we have a king bed and we tend to retreat to our corners; I get cold too easily and Finn throws the covers off. But, oddly, I don't mind. If he is holding me tight, I can't disappear.

I wait until he falls asleep, until I feel his breath falling in even puffs on the back of my shoulder. "I have to tell you something," I whisper. "Everything I dreamed in the hospital? I think it was . . . real."

There is no response.

"I was in the Galápagos," I say, testing the words out loud. "There was a man there."

Almost imperceptibly, Finn's arm tightens around me. I hold my breath.

"As long as you know who you're really having sex with," he murmurs.

He does not let go of me. And I do not sleep.

THIRTEEN

The next morning when Finn leaves for work, we do not talk about what I said in the middle of the night. He asks me a hundred times if I'm all right here on my own, and I spackle a smile on my face and tell him yes, and then the minute he walks out the door I have a panic attack.

What if I trip and fall?

What if I cough so hard I can't stop?

What if there's a fire and I can't move fast enough?

All I want to do is call Finn and tell him to come back, but it's both selfish and impossible.

So instead, I take Candis into the kitchen with me, leaning on the quad cane when I have to balance to get a mug from the cabinet. I fill up the kettle with water and put it on the stove, moving slowly and deliberately. I grind enough coffee for the Aeropress and congratulate myself on doing all this without stumbling. I slosh hot coffee all over my hand on the way to the table, and the first day of the rest of my life begins.

In the past, when Finn wasn't working tirelessly through a pandemic, we'd spend our days off lingering over coffee, reading *The New York Times* and *The Boston Globe* online. Finn would read aloud highlights about politics and sports. I gravitated toward the arts pages, and the obituaries. It sounds morbid, but it was actually for work: I kept a running list on my computer desktop of those who might have collections to be sold posthumously at Sotheby's.

Of course, I don't have a job at Sotheby's now. I don't know when or if I will again. Finn says I shouldn't worry about that; he thinks we can make do on his salary for a while if we are careful. But I have a feeling there are financial hurdles we're going to face that we can't even imagine yet. We are only a month into this pandemic.

The first *New York Times* banner I read: NYC DEATH TOLL SOARS PAST 10,000 IN REVISED VIRUS COUNT.

The *Boston Globe* headlines are only marginally less anxiety-producing: CHELSEA'S SPIKE IN CORONAVIRUS CASES CHALLENGES HOSPITALS AND STATE; BOSTON SCIENTIFIC GETS OK TO MAKE A LOW-COST VENTILATOR.

I click on the link to the obituaries.

Couple married more than 75 years dies within hours of each other: After Ernest and Moira Goldblatt got married in the summer of 1942, they spent the rest of their lives together, right up until the very end. On April 10, the couple passed away at the Hillside Nursing Home in Waltham, less than two hours apart. Moira, 96, had recently tested positive for Covid-19. Ernest, 100, had been sick but his test for the disease was still outstanding. In an effort to reduce the spread of the virus, nursing home residents who were infected were transferred to a separate space. But there was no doubt that the Goldblatts would be staying together.

I click to turn the page and scan the names. I click again.
And again.
Again.
There are twenty-six pages of obituaries today in *The Boston Globe*. With shaking hands, I close my computer.
There are already so many people who have lost someone, who'll

never receive another lopsided grin or smooth a cowlick or cry on a shoulder that smells like home. They'll always see the empty seat at a wedding, a birthday, breakfast.

Why did I survive, when those they loved didn't?

It's not like I did anything right—I don't even remember going to the hospital.

But it's also not like they did anything wrong.

I feel a crushing sense that if I am here, there has to be an explanation. Because the alternative—that this virus is random, that anyone and everyone could die—is so overwhelming that it is hard to breathe. Again.

I'm not conceited enough to think that I am special; I'm not religious enough to think I was spared by a higher power. I may not ever know why I'm still here and why the people in the rooms on either side of me at the hospital are not. But I can pivot on this point of the axis, and make sure whatever happens from here on in is worthy of this second chance I've been given.

I just don't know what that looks like, exactly.

I reopen my computer, and type into Google: *Jobs in art business.*

A string of them pop onto my screen: Senior Business Development Manager, Artsy. Adjunct faculty, Institute of Art. Creative Director, Omni Health Corp. Art Director—Business Banking Division, JPMorgan Chase.

All look equally uninspiring.

I truly enjoyed my work at Sotheby's. I loved the people I met and the art I helped sell.

Or at least that's what I'd told myself.

I let my mind drift back to the last time I saw Kitomi and her painting.

If I got sick that night, and if asymptomatic people can spread the virus—could I have infected her?

Panicked, I look her up online. As far as I can tell, she is still alive and well in New York with her painting.

I remember how it felt to stand in the presence of that kind of artistic greatness. In front of that Toulouse-Lautrec, my fingers had itched for a brush, even though I was no Toulouse-Lautrec, no Van Gogh. I was a competent artist, but not a great one, and I knew it. Like my father, I could make a decent copy—but that's different from creating an original masterpiece.

I had grown up in the shadow of my mother's prize-winning photography. So instead of trying to create my own legacy—and failing—I reshaped my skill set to fit a field adjacent to art.

I erase one word in the search bar.

Jobs in art.

Fashion designer. Animator. Art teacher. Illustrator. Tattoo artist. Interior designer. Motion graphics designer. Art therapist.

Art therapy is the practice of incorporating visual art media to improve cognitive and sensory-motor function, self-esteem, and emotional coping skills for mental health treatment.

Immediately I am back on a beach in Isabela, making tiny dolls out of flotsam and jetsam and setting them in a sandcastle with Beatriz. I am writing our names on lava rocks and making them part of a standing wall. I am explaining to her why monks make beautiful mandalas and then brush the sand away.

I've already been thinking of another career, without even realizing it. I've practiced it, with Beatriz.

I rub my hand over my face. I imagine filling out an application for admission to a graduate program in art therapy, listing my imaginary experience in the field.

But maybe that's the point. Maybe the Galápagos wasn't something that happened, but something that is *supposed* to happen.

When it starts to feel like a chicken-and-egg logic bomb, I decide that I have done enough job searching for the day. Instead, I open up Instagram and see college friends giving thumbs-up on planes, cashing in on cheap vacation deals. Another friend has posted a picture of her aunt, who died yesterday of Covid, with a long tribute. A celebrity I follow is doing a fundraiser for Broadway Cares/Equity Fights AIDS. My former neighbor posts a teary video about postponing her wedding when they were totally going to do it in a *safe way*. It's like there are two different realities unfolding at the same time.

I do not post often on Facebook, but I have an account. When I open it, there are dozens of notifications from acquaintances: *Sending healing thoughts! I'm praying for you, Diana. You got this.*

Frowning, I click onto the post that inspired these comments. Finn must have logged in to my account, because he's written a short paragraph explaining that I have been hospitalized with Covid and put on a ventilator.

I tamp down the annoyance at the thought of him logging in as me.

The comments are supportive, effusive, heartfelt. Some are political, claiming that the virus is a hoax and I have the flu. Other friends attack that poster on my behalf. All this while I was unconscious.

On a whim, I type *Covid-19 survivors* into the search tab, and a string of articles comes up, as well as a list of support groups. Most are private, but I dive into one that is not and start reading through the timeline.

Has anyone else found their taste has changed? I used to love spicy, and now not so much. Plus, everything smells like bacon.

Sleep is impossible—getting migraines every night.

Am I the only one losing hair? I had long, thick curls and now my hair's super thin; how long will this last?

Hang in there, someone else has responded. *Mine's stopped falling out!*

Try zinc.

Try vitamin D.

Tested positive 3/11, tested positive again on day 10, still testing positive a month later—is it safe for me to be around people?

Question for the ones who have had Covid-19: have y'all been getting nosebleeds on just one side?

Can I get this virus again if I've already had it?

My doctor won't believe me when I say that I didn't have heart palpitations before . . .

I am getting more and more freaked out. What if leaving the hospital is only just the start? What if I have long-term effects that haven't even shown up yet?

to feel concentrated and acute, personal. Whatever we forfeit echoes the pain from all the other times we have been disappointed in our lives. When I was sedated and I thought I had lost my mother, it was amplified by all the times she left me when I was little.

She looks up and finds me watching her. I do that, now, trying to see myself in the curve of her jaw or the texture of her hair. "Have you ever been to Mexico?" she asks.

I shake my head. "I'd like to go, one day. It's on my bucket list."

Her face lights up. "What else is on there?"

"The Galápagos," I say softly.

"I've been," she replies. "That poor tortoise—Lonesome George. He died."

I was the one to tell her that, a day before my life changed. "So I hear." I lean back on my elbows, glancing at her through the screen. She is pixelated and whole at the same time. "Did you always want to travel?" I ask.

"When I was a girl," my mother says, "we went nowhere. My father was a cattle farmer and he used to say you can't take a vacation from the cows. One day an encyclopedia salesman came to the house and I begged my parents to subscribe. Every month there was a new volume showing me a world a lot bigger than McGregor, Iowa."

I am entranced. I try to connect the dots between her childhood and her move to New York City.

"The best part was that we got a bonus book—an atlas," she adds. "There weren't computers back then, you know. To see what it looked like thousands of feet up a mountain in Tibet or down in the rice paddies of Vietnam or even just the Golden Gate Bridge in San Francisco—I wanted to be there. All the places. I wanted to put myself in the frame." She shrugs. "So I did."

My mother, I realize, mapped out her life literally. I did mine figuratively. But it was for the same reason—to make sure I didn't get trapped someplace I didn't want to be.

I don't know what makes me ask the next question. Maybe it is because I have never struck a tuning fork in myself and heard it resonate in my mother; maybe it's because I have spent so many years blaming her for not sharing her life with me, even though I never actually asked her to do so. But I sit up, legs crossed, and say, "Do you have children?"

A small frown forms between her brows, and she closes the photo album. Her hands smooth over its cover, nails catching at the embossed gold words. A LIFE, it says. Banal, and also spot-on.

"I do," my mother says, just when I think she will not answer. "I *did*."

Let this go, I tell myself. Alzheimer's 101 says do not remind a person with dementia of a memory or event that might be upsetting.

She meets my gaze through the screen. "I . . . don't know," she says.

But the cloudiness that is the hallmark of her illness isn't what I see in her eyes. It's the opposite—the memory of a relationship that wasn't what it might have been, even if you do not know why.

It's blinking at your surroundings, and not knowing how you got to this point.

And I am just as guilty of it as she is.

I've spent so much time dissecting how different my mother and I are that I never bothered to consider what we have in common.

"I'm tired," my mother says.

"You should lie down," I tell her. I gather up my blanket.

"Thank you for visiting," she says politely.

"Thank you for letting me," I reply, just as gracious. "Don't forget to lock the slider."

I wait until she is inside her apartment, but even in the space of those few seconds, she's forgotten to secure the latch. I could tell her a million times; she will likely never remember.

While I'm waiting for my Uber, I laugh softly at my foolishness. At first, I thought maybe I'd come back to this world so that I could give my mother a second chance.

Now I'm starting to think I'm here so she can give *me* one.

Every night at seven P.M., New Yorkers lean out their windows and bang pots and pans for the frontline workers to hear, In a show of support. Sometimes Finn hears them when he is headed home from work.

On those days, he comes into the apartment and strips and showers and goes right to the cabinet over the refrigerator to take out a bottle of Macallan whiskey. He pours himself a glass and sometimes doesn't even speak to me until he's drunk it.

I didn't know Finn even liked whiskey.

Each night, the amount he pours gets a little bigger. He is careful to leave enough in the bottle for the next night. Sometimes he passes out on the couch and I have to help him to bed.

During the day, when he's at work, I climb on a step stool and take out the Macallan. I pour some of the whiskey down the sink. Not an amount that would raise suspicion; just enough for me to protect him a little from himself.

By the end of May we aren't washing the groceries anymore or waiting to open our mail, but we're freaked out about slipstreams, and whether you can catch the virus from a jogger who runs past you. I start receiving the unemployment benefits I became eligible for when I was furloughed, but they certainly don't cover my half of the rent.

When I start to feel like I'm going stir-crazy, I remind myself of how lucky I am. I scour forums of long-haul Covid survivors, who are still suffering weeks later with symptoms no one understands and no doctors have the bandwidth or knowledge to address. I read articles about women who are balancing work and online education for their kids; and profiles of frontline workers who get paid scandalously little to risk their exposure to the virus. I see Finn stagger in after his long shifts, haunted by what he's seen. Sometimes it feels like the whole world is holding its breath. If we don't gasp, soon, we will all pass out.

One Saturday when Finn has the day off, we spend the afternoon getting back to ground zero: cleaning the apartment, doing laundry, sorting through the mail that has piled up. We play Rock Paper Scissors to choose chores, which leaves me scrubbing toilets while Finn fishes through piles of envelopes and junk mail for the cable bill and the bank statements. Every time I pass by him at the kitchen table, I feel ashamed. Usually we split the cost of utilities and rent, but with my contributions reduced to a trickle, he's paying the lion's share.

He picks up a stack of glossy catalogs he has separated out from the bills and tosses them into the milk crate we use as a recycling bin. "I don't know why we keep getting these," he says. "College brochures."

"No, wait." I put down my dustrag and sift through them, pulling a bunch back out and cradling them in one arm. "They're for me." I meet his gaze. "I'm thinking of going back to school."

He blinks at me. "For *what*? You already have a master's in art business."

"I might change careers," I tell him. "I want to find out more about art therapy."

"How are you paying for tuition?" Finn asks.

It stings. "I have some savings."

He doesn't respond, but implicit in his look is: *You may not by the time this is over.*

It makes me feel equally guilty—for wanting to spend money on myself when I haven't been carrying my own weight on household expenses, and angry—because he's right. "I just feel like this could be . . . a wake-up call."

"You're not the only one who lost a job, Di."

I shake my head. "Not only getting furloughed. *Everything.* There has to be a reason that I got sick."

Finn suddenly looks very, very tired. "There doesn't have to be a reason. Viruses don't need reasons. They strike. Randomly."

"Well, I can't believe that." I lift my chin. "I can't believe I'm alive because of the luck of the draw."

He stares at me for another moment, and then shakes his head and mutters something I don't hear. He rips open another envelope and eviscerates its contents.

"Why are you mad?" I ask.

Finn pushes his chair away from the table. "I'm not mad," he says. "But, I mean—going back to school? Changing *careers*? I can't believe you didn't happen to mention this anytime over the last month."

I blurt out, "I've been visiting my mother."

"Wow," Finn says quietly. Betrayal is written all over the margins of his face.

"I didn't say anything because . . . I thought you'd tell me not to go."

His eyes narrow, as if he is searching to find me. "I would have gone with you," he says. "You have to be careful."

"You think I could get hurt taking the trash into the hallway to dump it."

"My point exactly. You shouldn't be doing that, either. You're only a month out of rehab—"

"You treat me like I'm on the verge of dying," I snap.

"Because you *were*," Finn counters, rising from his chair.

We are standing a foot apart, both of us crackling with frustration.

He wants to gently set me down exactly where I was before this happened, like he's been holding that place for me in a board game, and we are going to pick up where we left off. The problem is that I'm not the same player.

"When I thought you were going to die," Finn says, "I didn't believe there could be anything more awful than a world you weren't in. But this is worse, Diana. This is you, in the world, not letting me be a part of it." His eyes are dark, desperate. "I don't know what I did wrong."

Immediately, I reach out, my hands catching his. "You've done nothing wrong," I say, because it is true.

The relief in his eyes nearly breaks me. Finn's arms come around my waist. "You want to go back to school?" he says. "We'll figure out how. You want a PhD? I'll be in the front row at your dissertation defense. We've always wanted the same things, Di. If this is a detour on the way to everything we've dreamed about, that's okay."

A detour. Inside, where he cannot see, I flinch.

What if I don't want what I used to?

"What did you want to be when you grew up?" I murmur.

A laugh startles out of Finn. "A magician."

I'm charmed. "Really? Why?"

"Because they made things appear out of thin air," Finn says, with a shrug. "Something from nothing. How cool is that?"

I nestle close to him. "I would have come to all your shows. I would have been that annoying superfan."

"I would have promoted you to magician's assistant." He grins. "Would you have let me saw you in half?"

"Anytime," I tell him.

But I think: *That is the easy part. The trick is in putting me back together.*

The next morning, I video-call Rodney and tell him that Finn doesn't want me to go back to school. "Remind me why you need his permission?" he says.

"Because it changes things, when you're a couple. Like how much we can pay in rent, if I'm not making a salary. Or how much time we'll actually spend together."

"You hardly spend any time together now. He's a resident."

"Well, anyway, I didn't call to talk to you. Is Rayanne there?"

Rodney frowns. "No, she's working."

"Like . . . doing a reading for someone?"

"Nursing home," he says. "The only thing that pays worse than a career in art is being a psychic." His eyes widen. "*That's* why you want to talk to her."

"What if I'm being an idiot, thinking about starting over now? Finn could be right. This could be some weird reaction to having a second chance, or something."

Rodney slowly puts it all together. "So you want Rayanne to take a peek a few years out and tell you if you're gluing pom-poms together with kids who have anxiety from gluten allergies—"

"—That is *not* art therapy—"

"—or if you're wearing stilettos and in Eva's old office? Mmnope. It doesn't work that way."

"Easy for you to say," I tell him, pressing my hand to my forehead. "Nothing makes sense, Rodney. *Nothing*. I know Finn thinks that I shouldn't make any radical changes, because I've been through so much. Instead of trying new things, I should find the stuff that feels comfortable."

Rodney looks at me. "Oh my God. Nothing bad's ever happened to you before."

I scowl at him. "That's not true."

"Okay, sure, you had a mother who didn't know you existed, but your daddy still doted on you. Maybe you had to go to your second-choice college. You had a share of white lady problems, but nothing that's knocked the ground out from under your feet. Until you caught Covid, and now you understand that sometimes shit happens you can't control."

I feel anger bubbling inside me. "What is your point?"

"You know I'm from Louisiana," Rodney says. "And that I'm Black and gay."

My lips twitch. "I'd noticed."

"I have spent a great deal of time pretending to be someone that other people want me to be," he says. "You don't need a crystal ball, honey. You need a good hard look at *right now*."

My jaw drops open.

Rodney scoffs. "Rayanne's got nothing on me," he says.

In late May, the strict lockdown of the city is eased. As the weather improves, the streets become busier. It's still different—everyone is masked; restaurant service is solely outdoors—but it feels a little less like a demilitarized zone.

I get stronger, able to go up and down stairs without having to stop halfway. When Finn is at the hospital, I take walks from our place on the Upper East Side through Central Park, going further south and west every day. The more people venture outside, the more I tailor my outings to odd times of the day—just before dawn, or when everyone else is home eating dinner. There are still people out, but it's easier to social-distance from them.

Early one morning I put on my leggings and sneakers and strike off for the reservoir in Central Park. It's my favorite walk, and I know it is because it makes me remember another static body of water and a thicket of brush. If I close my eyes and listen to the woodcock and the sparrows, I can pretend they are finches and mockingbirds.

This is exactly what I'm doing when I hear someone call my name. "Diana? Is that you?"

On the running path, wearing a black tracksuit and a paisley mask and her trademark purple glasses, is Kitomi Ito.

"Yes!" I say, stepping forward before I remember that we are not allowed to touch, to hug. "You're still here."

She laughs. "Haven't shuffled off the mortal coil yet, no."

"I mean, you haven't moved."

"That, too," Kitomi says. She nods toward the path. "Walk a bit?"

I fall into step, six feet away.

"I admit I thought I would have heard from you by now," she says.

"Sotheby's furloughed me," I tell her. "They furloughed almost everyone."

"Ah, well, that explains why no one's been beating down the door asking for the painting." She tilts her head. "Isn't the big sale this month?"

It is, but it has never crossed my mind.

"I must say, I've never been more grateful for a decision than I was to not auction the Toulouse-Lautrec. For weeks now, it's just been the two of us in the apartment. I would have been quite lonely, without it."

I understand what she's talking about. I was just staring at a manmade reservoir, after all, and pretending it was a lagoon in the Galápagos. I could close my eyes and hear Beatriz splashing and Gabriel teasing me to dive in.

customers, and barefoot kids kicking a soccer ball. It has the lazy, boozy atmosphere of a tourist town, and I'm not the only person dragging a little roller bag down the gritty dust of the street.

A Gordian knot of iguanas untangles and scatters when the wheels of my bag get too close. I check my phone for the address of Casa del Cielo, but the hotels are all arranged in a neat line, like sparkling white teeth along the edge of the ocean. Mine is small—a boutique. Its stucco reflects the sun, and a blue mosaic sign spells out its name.

It looks nothing like the hotel I dreamed.

When I walk up to the front, there is a couple leaving. They hold the door for me, and I pull my bag inside and approach the front desk.

The air-conditioning blows over me as I give my name. The clerk, a college-age kid, has dyed white-blond hair and a nose ring. He speaks perfect English. "Have you ever visited before?" he asks, when I hand him my credit card.

"Not really," I tell him, and he grins.

"That sounds like a story."

"It is," I say.

He gives me a room key, affixed to a little piece of polished coconut shell. "The Wi-Fi code is on the back," he says. "It's a little unreliable."

I can't help it; I laugh.

"If there's anything you need, just dial zero," he says.

I thank him and reach for the handle of my bag. Just before I get to the elevator, I turn around. "Does someone named Elena work here?" I ask.

He shakes his head. "Not that I know of . . ."

"That's okay," I tell him. "I must have been mistaken."

I wrote my master's thesis on the reliability of memory, and how it fails us. In Japan, there are monuments called tsunami stones—giant tablets on the coastline that warn descendants of earlier settlers not to build their homes past a certain point. They date back to 1896, when two tsunamis killed 22,000 people. The Japanese believe that it takes three generations to forget. Those who experience a trauma pass it along to their children and their grandchildren, and then the memory fades. To the survivors of a tragedy, that's unthinkable—what's the point of living through something terrible if you cannot convey the lessons you've learned? Since nothing will ever replace all you've lost, the only way to make meaning is to make sure no one else goes through what you did. Memories are the safeguards we use to keep from making the same mistakes.

In my art therapy practice, I started working with people whose lives had been affected in different ways by Covid—those who'd lost jobs or loved ones, or those who'd survived the virus and (like me) were left wondering why. Over the course of the past three years, my patients and I have created three pandemic stones—ten feet high by three feet wide, painted and carved by survivors with images and words that call forth the wisdom they have now, which they didn't have back then. There are pictures of stick figure families, some grayed out by death. There are mantras: *Find your joy. No job is worth killing yourself for.* There are images of Black fists raised in solidarity, of a globe in the shape of a heart, of a syringe filled with stars. The first one that we finished was installed in the lobby of the MoMA on the most recent anniversary of the pandemic.

The obelisk sits three floors below one of my mother's photos.

Exploring Isabela is a little bit like revisiting a city you toured when you were high as a kite. Some things look exactly the way I remember—like the flat black of the *pahoehoe* lava and the elbow of beach beyond the hotel. These must have been photographs I saw when I was planning my trip there that embedded themselves some-where in my subconscious, enough for me to call them up with le-gitimacy. But other pieces of the island are startlingly different, like the place the pangas come with their daily fishing catch, and the ar-chitecture of the small houses that freckle the road leading out of town. Abuela's little home, with the basement apartment, simply does not exist.

Tomorrow, I will arrange to take a tour of the island. I want to see the volcano and the trillizos. But right now, because it's been a long flight and I want to stretch my legs, I change into shorts and sneakers and a tank top, pull my hair into a ponytail, and walk down to the water's edge. I take off my shoes and wade up to my knees, watching Sally Lightfoot crabs polka-dot the rocks. I put my hands on my hips and look up at the clouds, then across the ocean at a small island that never existed in my dream. I breathe deeply, thinking that last time I was here, I couldn't breathe at all.

I sit on a rock with an iguana that is completely unbothered by the company and wait for my feet to dry before putting on my sneakers again. This time, I start jogging away from town. Another thing that looks nothing like it did in my imagination: the entrance to the tortoise breeding ground. It's touristy, with signs and maps and cartoon pictures of eggs and hatching tortoises.

There's a couple leaving; they smile at me as I pass them on my way in. "It's closed," the woman says, "but you can still see the babies in the pens outside."

"Thanks," I say, and I walk toward the horseshoe of enclosures. Beneath cacti, tortoises huddle together, stretching their old-man necks toward whatever danger lies six inches ahead. One unhinges his jaw and sticks out a triangular pink tongue.

The tortoises are arranged in size order. Some pens have only two or three, others are crammed. The babies are no bigger than my fist, and they are clambering over each other, creating their own obstacle course.

One of the little ones manages to get its feet on the shell of another, double-stacked for a breathtaking moment before it topples over onto its back.

Its feet are pedaling in the air, its head snicked back inside its shell.

I look around, wondering if there's an attendant who will flip this poor little guy back over.

Well. They're babies; they can't be dangerous.

The retaining wall is only thigh-high. I put my foot on it, intending to climb over, complete a rescue mission, and leave.

I have no idea why the sole of my sneaker slips.

"Cuidado!"

I feel a hand grab my wrist the moment before I fall.

And I turn.

Author's Note

Humans mark tragedy. Everyone remembers where they were when Kennedy was shot, when the Twin Towers fell, and the last thing they did before the world shut down due to the Covid-19 pandemic.

I was at a wedding in Tulum. The bride was an actress who—in a month—was going to star in the off-Broadway musical adaptation of *Between the Lines,* a novel I co-wrote with my daughter. I attended her wedding with the librettist and his husband, and our director and his husband. We all sat together at a table, drank margaritas, and had a wonderful time. From there, I met up with my husband in Aspen, where my son was about to propose to his girlfriend. There was buzz about coronavirus, but it didn't seem real.

Then we got notice at our hotel that a guest had tested positive. By the time we flew home, New Hampshire was going into lockdown. My last trip to a grocery store was March 11, 2020 (and as of this moment, I still haven't gone to one since). One week later I learned that all of the other people at my table at the wedding in Mexico had contracted Covid. Two were hospitalized.

I never caught it.

I have asthma, and I took quarantine very seriously. I can count on one hand the number of times I've left my house in the past year—

us he ran for the Jeep, scooped me into his arms, and dragged my mother with him to the cellar hatch. My mother was already fiddling with her camera. "But I need to—"

"No," my father yelled. "You do not."

Mrs. Evans followed us down there, still muttering about *that fool Vietnam Tim*. She sat down and tuned a little battery-powered radio to a station that was repeating the tornado emergency signal. We tucked ourselves between boxes of storage. Suddenly Vietnam Tim threw open the hatch doors. His eyes were wild, his hair electric. "It's gonna reverse direction," he yelled down. "A one-two punch."

"Come down here before you get killed," my father said.

Vietnam Tim grinned. "And miss all the fun?" He closed the metal doors.

Even with my head buried against my father's chest, I could hear the tornado. It sounded like a hundred trains clattering on the same track. I heard glass shattering and car alarms and fire alarms and house alarms and then the monkey shriek of Nitpick.

That's when Mrs. Evans lost it. She tossed aside the radio and raced up the ladder, throwing open the metal doors and trying to get to the barn.

"Fuck," my father said. He put me down on the floor and looked at me and then my mother. "Do not move." And then he took off after her.

I screamed for him, but my voice was carried away by the wind. My mother stood up and calmly climbed the wooden steps that led out of the open cellar hatch, like a queen walking to her beheading. She stood half in and half out of the cellar, looking out at Vietnam Tim with his chin pointed to the sky. "That's the cold front," he cried. "It's gonna shift back again."

Just as quickly as it had started, everything went still.

Between-heartbeats still. Hold-your-breath still.

Vietnam Tim's hair fluttered to lay flat against his scalp again. The wind disappeared. My mother walked outside, and I followed her, like I was tied by a thread.

The gazebo in the front yard was just . . . missing. The flowerpots were smashed and all the windows on the first floor of the inn had shattered. The twister was distant, undulating, like it was plotting its next move.

"Is it over?" I whispered.

My mother didn't look at me. "Yes," she breathed. "And no."

The leaves at my feet started dancing as the wind picked up pace. The barn door opened, and my father came out, one arm braced around Mrs. Evans, who was sobbing.

Another tornado siren pierced the silence. My feet felt like they were rising, like I was a balloon.

Vietnam Tim locked eyes with my mother. "Wanna go chase it?" he asked.

"Hannah," my father cried.

She turned to him, her face wide open, as if we couldn't already see the parts of her that were missing.

How could you ask me to choose?

She was moving toward the blue Jeep before I could grab for her. My father bolted into action, snatching me into his free arm and dragging me and Mrs. Evans to the cellar again, even though the wind had risen so fast that it felt like we were pushing against an invisible wall.

We tumbled inside to safety. As my father struggled to close the hatch, I saw the Jeep drive off, moments before the entire barn was flung into the sky.

———·———

It took four minutes for the world to be destroyed again.

———·———

When my father and I went looking for her, hand in hand, the ground was covered with ice crunching under my feet. But it turned out it wasn't hail, it was glass. Shrapnel and splinters and the spoils of a war, the enemy long gone.

The town of Ochelata was a war zone, but it had been a discriminating battle. The side of the street with Pete's bar on it had been demolished. The restaurant, on the other side, remained pristine and untouched. Some houses we passed had no glass in the windows anymore, others had trees upended with the roots now scraping the sky. Some were missing porches, fences, roofs. Others looked exactly like they had this morning.

The home beside the Next of Inn had been completely ripped off its foundation, and reset gently in the middle of the street.

We returned to the inn without my mother. Mrs. Evans was sitting on the porch. "Has she—" my father asked, and the innkeeper just shook her head.

I wandered to the fence where I'd stood with Vietnam Tim; it was still intact. I wanted to blink and wake up in a world where the past two days had never happened.

I rested my forehead on the flat railing and felt a tug on my shirt, plus a hot gust of air. When I looked up, Nitpick was eating the hem.

But before I could tell Mrs. Evans, the blue Jeep drove up. Vietnam Tim got out from the driver's side and executed a little bow. "I hate to say I told you so, but I told you so."

By the time my mother unfolded herself from the passenger seat, her face glowing and her eyes snapping with excitement, I was already racing toward her. I threw my arms around her waist, hugging her so close you couldn't sew a seam between us.

My father walked toward us, an inferno.

"Paul," my mother said gently, soothing. "What's important is that I'm fine. That we're all fine."

A muscle ticked in his jaw. "Is that really what you think is important?"

"But the photos—wait till you see—"

"This was a mistake," my father said. "Coming here. Us. All of it." He took me, peeling me off my mother, and stuffing me into the rental car.

"Paul? Where are you going?" My mother took three steps toward us. *"Paul?"*

"See how you like it," he said.

The sedan screamed out of the inn's driveway, fishtailing. If I needed any more proof that the world as I knew it had unraveled, this was it.

My father was the one running away, instead of my mother.

———·———

I knew, in the way that kids do, to let the silence ride shotgun. It wasn't until we were driving for an hour on the old Route 66 that I finally asked where we were going. "You know," my father said, huffing a laugh, "I have no idea."

We'd just reached Catoosa when we saw the Blue Whale from the road. My father looked at me and I looked at him and by unspoken agreement, he drove right up to it—this weird, aqua-painted concrete whale half submerged at the edge of a little pond. I didn't think I'd ever seen anything quite so sad before—a landlocked fake whale in the middle of Oklahoma.

It looked like a minigolf sculpture without a putting green, like a kids' papier-mâché version of a cetacean. There was a gift store that was closed, but we could still walk right through the mouth of the whale into its boardwalk belly. There were signs saying no swimming was allowed, but at one point it must have been—there was a ladder and a slide right into the brackish water.

My father stepped up to a little plaque. "After noticing kids playing in a pond near his property, Hugh Davis built the blue whale in 1972 as an anniversary present for his wife, with a swim dock for local children. It became a major hub for people traveling across Route 66. When Davis died, the whale fell into disrepair, until his son Blaine restored it in 1988."

I stared into the painted eye of the creature, which seemed to be saying it knew it was stuck somewhere it was never meant to be.

My father lightly kicked at one of the cement teeth, his hands in his pockets. "Maybe I should have built her a whale," he said.

———·———

We drove back to the Next of Inn through Ochelata, which was slowly piecing itself back together. Mrs. Evans wasn't there, but she had left us peanut butter and jelly sandwiches to eat for dinner. I ate slowly while my father told my mother that we would be flying home the next day.

That night I woke up from a nightmare where I was doing a word search, and all of the letters kept sliding off the page. I tried to fall asleep again, but this time I dreamed that we were back in New York, and our apartment was nothing but splinters of wood.

My parents were not in their bed. The bathroom door was ajar and a slice of lemon light fell onto the carpet from inside. I could hear their voices over the soft rush of the faucet.

I didn't think you'd be back, my mother said.

I'm not the one who leaves. That's you.

What do you want me to say, Paul?

There was a hiccup of silence.

That you'll come home with us, he said. *That you'll stay home.*

I padded down the stairs and peered out the window beside the front door, which was no longer a window but an open space. The glass had been swept up from the floor, so I had a clear view of the night sky, stars suddenly close enough to touch, like sparks thrown from a fire.

There was also a red ember dancing in the dark. I pushed open the screen door and saw Vietnam Tim sitting on the wicker rocker, smoking a cigarette. "Hey," he said, seeing me. He waved the cigarette toward me. "Want one?" Then he winced. "That's probably like the cursing," he realized.

"Yeah. . . . I'm leaving tomorrow," I said.

"What a coincidence," Vietnam Tim replied. "So am I."

"Where will you go?"

He waved his arm, the bright red tip of the cigarette drawing a loop in the night. "Wherever the winds take me," he said.

"I'm going back to New York," I told him. "I may never leave there again."

His teeth flashed, a lightning smile. "So much for apples not falling far from trees," Vietnam Tim answered.

In the morning, Vietnam Tim had left without saying goodbye, and I realized that my mother was not joining us to go to the airport. Instead, she was going to spend a few more days in Ochelata, photographing the devastation of the EF4 tornado. She would chronicle the absence of homes where they had stood hours before, and the empty arms of mothers who had lost children, piles of debris that had been family businesses and churches. The images would eventually include a Jenga heap of broken beams with the town population sign cracked down the middle; another of a horse rearing as it was being recaptured from the school gymnasium where it had taken frantic refuge; a dog's paw emerging from a mountain of rubble; and Mrs. Evans, staring at the remains of her broken barn, her arm hooked around the neck of Nitpick. This series, Broken Things, would eventually be featured at the International Center of Photography, and won my mother a World Press Photo award.

Before we left, my mother hugged me. "I'll be home soon," she promised, but she looked at my father as she said it. "I can't leave before I finish the job."

"I thought you were here for the rain," I said.

"That *was* the job," my mother agreed. "But now it's something else."

It was always something else.

I watched my mother tentatively move toward my father, and even more tentatively come close enough for her to brush her lips against his. There was only a second of hesitation, and then he kissed her back.

I fed Nitpick one last apple while my father put our suitcases into the rental car. As we drove to the airport I thought about something Vietnam Tim had said, when I asked him how a tornado ends.

The cold air above it breaks apart, he had told me. *Or the storm just gets all ropy and weak.*

In other words, one side gives up.

At the airport, the gate agent who checked us in looked at my passport. "Happy birthday!" she sang, all teeth, something my own mother hadn't remembered to say.

The panic attack hit just as the plane leveled after takeoff.

What if a tornado comes now?

What if the plane just falls out of the sky?

What if the ground swallows us whole?

I started shaking so hard that my father, who was in the seat beside me with his eyes closed, felt it. He covered my hand with his. "What's wrong, Diana?"

What I meant to say: *Everything.*

What came out: "I don't want her to come home."

His fingers stilled over mine, and then squeezed. "Of course you do," he said, as if I'd just told him the sky is green when it obviously is blue.

I turned away from him, feeling betrayed. If anyone should understand, it would be him.

A fly that had stowed away on this flight buzzed in front of me, landing on the window. I watched it bat up against the thick glass, over and over, like it only now realized it had made a colossal mistake and wanted to be on the other side.

Because we had just flown in and it was my birthday, my father let me pick the take-out food. We ate Thai from the place I loved, where they always gave us free dumplings. My father scooped ice cream from a carton in the freezer and put a birthday candle in it and sang to me and we both pretended we were happy.

He told me I could unpack tomorrow after school, but I liked things in their proper places. So before I went to bed, I unzipped my little suitcase, planning to put my dirty clothes in the hamper and hang up the ones that needed to go in the closet.

On top of my clothes there was a folded note addressed in my mother's handwriting.

Happy birthday, Diana, it said on the outside.

Inside was a list.